THE CONSIDINE CURSE

GARETH P. JONES

BLOOMSBURY
LONDON OXFORD NEW YORK NEW DELHI SYDNEY

Bloomsbury Publishing, London, Oxford, New York, New Delhi and Sydney

First published in Great Britain in August 2011
by Bloomsbury Publishing Plc
50 Bedford Square, London WC1B 3DP

www.bloomsbury.com

Bloomsbury is a registered trademark of Bloomsbury Publishing Plc

A CIP catalogue record for this book is available from the British Library

ISBN 978 1 4088 1151 1

Typeset by Hewer Text UK Ltd, Edinburgh
Printed and bound in Great Britain by CPI Group (UK) Ltd, Croydon CR0 4YY

For my seven cousins –
Debbie, Richard, Emma, Mark
Kate, Catrin and Marc

1

THE ARRIVAL

The snow seemed so clean and white from the aeroplane window but underfoot it is grey and slushy. It soaks through the thin material of my trainers and seeps into my socks. When I grumble about my feet, Mum claims she told me to wear sensible shoes but I only remember her saying to wrap up warmly.

I spot the church steeple above a row of houses and step into an icy puddle. I feel miserable. My nose and hands are cold but my body is hot under my heavy winter coat. We turn a corner and see the church. There are cars outside.

'I told you we could have parked nearer,' I say.

'I needed a walk to clear my head before we arrived,' Mum replies.

'Yeah, and I really needed to wash my feet,' I mutter.

Mum looks at my soaked shoes. 'I'm sorry, love. It's

just that I've been so nervous about seeing them again after all this time.'

'At least you've met them before. I've got to meet a whole bunch of people I'm supposed to be related to that I never even knew existed until last week.'

Five days ago, I came in from school to find Mum sitting by the phone in tears. When I put my arm round her and asked her what was wrong, I was expecting her to tell me that she had split up with her latest boyfriend, which is what it normally is.

Instead she replied, 'That was my little brother, Will. My mother died yesterday.'

'You've got a brother?' was the only thing I could think of to say.

'I've got five brothers,' she admitted, avoiding my gaze.

'I've got *five* uncles?' I squawked.

'I don't think you heard me, Mariel. My mother has died.'

'I did hear you. *My* grandmother is dead and somehow her death has magically produced five uncles.'

'This is not a good time for your flippancy, Mariel. I told Will we'd fly over for the funeral. I'll look into flights and call your school tomorrow.'

'So all my life you've lied to me,' I said, unwilling to let this one go.

'I didn't lie. I just didn't tell you the whole truth,' she

said, which in itself was a lie because she told me she was an only child.

'Five uncles,' I repeated, still taking it in. 'And how many other relatives have you kept hidden from me?'

'No more. That's it,' she said. 'Well, they all have wives and children,' she added.

'I've got cousins?' I said.

'Seven, I think. Harkett's got two boys, Sewell has two girls, Kitson's got Amelia, Robson's got Freddie, and Will and Chrissie have just had a baby called Madeleine.'

I couldn't believe how casually she said it like it wasn't a massive deal. I still can't believe it.

'How could you keep all this secret from me?' I demanded.

She looked at me the way she does when she thinks I am going on and said, 'Can we talk about this later, Mariel? I need to not cry for a bit.'

That was five days ago. She has cried every day since then and I am no closer to understanding why she kept my family secret from me all this time.

She pushes open the wooden gate and we enter the churchyard where I find another reason to be annoyed with her.

'I said everyone would be wearing black,' I say.

'Don't be so conventional,' she replies.

It's easy for her to say that. While she is wearing a

black pullover and skirt, she told me that my navy blue dress would be fine. Now, as I approach the relatives I have never met, who are *all* dressed in black, I feel even more out of place than before. Mum points out my uncles and aunts standing by the church door but I have noticed what must be my cousins in a corner of the churchyard. There are six of them: three boys and three girls of varying age and size. One of my uncles spots us and comes over.

'Will,' says Mum, hugging him.

'I'm glad you came. It's been too long,' he says. He turns to me. 'And this must be Mariel. Hi, I'm your Uncle Will.' He offers me his hand.

I say hello. He seems nice. He is younger than Mum and has dimples that show when he smiles.

'Where's Chrissie? I'm dying to meet her,' says Mum.

'She's taken Madeleine straight to Mum's place,' he replies. 'They'll be at the wake but we were worried Madeleine would cry during the service. She's normally good as gold but you know what babies are like as soon as you need them to be quiet.'

'Mariel bawled her eyes out all through Dad's funeral.'

'I remember,' says Will. He turns to me. 'That's the last time I saw you. You've grown a bit since then,' he says, and he winks at me in a friendly way. 'How long are you here for?'

'Ten days,' Mum replies. 'We've booked a room in a hotel in Chilton.'

'I told you on the phone we'd all be happy to put you up,' says Will.

Mum reacts to this with a loud sob that draws the attention of my other uncles and aunts, although my cousins remain deep in conversation, undisturbed by the noise.

'Sorry, Will,' says Mum. 'It's just been so long . . .'

I feel embarassed by Mum's outburst. Will puts his arm around Mum's shoulder to comfort her. 'Mariel, why don't you go and say hello to your cousins?' he says.

I look over at them.

'They're not as intimidating as they look,' he adds. 'Amelia and Freddie are your age and Oberon's only a year older.'

Although I'm not exactly wild about the idea of introducing myself to a bunch of complete strangers, I am more than happy to let someone else deal with Mum for a change, so I approach my cousins cautiously. They are huddled together and talking so quietly that, even as I near, I can't catch a word they are saying. They are so engrossed in their conversation they fail to notice me until I am standing right behind them.

The oldest and tallest boy sees me and coughs to alert the others to my presence. He is awkward-looking, with glasses and a long face. The others stop talking and all turn to look at me. As their six faces stare silently at me I see that they all have the same intense dark brown, almost black, eyes. Mine are blue like Mum's.

'This is a family funeral,' says a fat boy with reddish brown hair.

'For our grandmother,' adds an extremely pretty girl who is about my age but wearing more make-up than I'm allowed to wear.

'I'm your cousin, Mariel,' I say.

'You're not a Considine,' says the fat boy incredulously.

'She's Aunt Lynda's daughter,' says a girl, younger than me, with thick black hair that falls like a curtain across half of her face.

'Ah, the long lost cousin from Austray-lia,' says one of the boys, in what I guess is supposed to be an Australian accent. He is good-looking, with an athletic build and a head of messy hair.

'So she's one of us?' says the pretty girl.

'She's no Considine,' repeats the fat one.

'Hello? I am here you know,' I say angrily.

'She talks funny. She's only a half-cousin,' says the youngest of them, a girl with pigtails who looks around eight or nine but whose eyes seem much older.

'Are all English people this rude or is it just my blood relatives?' I ask. 'And there's no such thing as a half-cousin. Flora was my grandma too.'

'The Considine blood runs through our veins, but everybody's blood is not the same,' the young girl hisses. 'The children of the sons, we are the ones. Not the child of the daughter, with blood like water.'

I have no idea what to say to this and am glad when the good-looking boy laughs and offers his hand. 'Sorry about her. Elspeth loves her poetry. I'm Freddie,' he says brightly. 'Please forgive us. We're all so upset about Grandma's death we forgot our manners.'

He doesn't sound upset to me. I smile. 'I'm Mariel,' I say, even though I have already introduced myself.

'This is Gerald and Oberon.' Freddie points at the tall, awkward-looking boy and the fat one.

'Hello,' says Gerald. It's the first thing he has said.

Oberon leans forward and his nose twitches as though he is sniffing me.

'And this is Lily,' continues Freddie, gesturing towards the shy-looking girl with the curtain of black hair standing next to the youngest girl, who I can see now is her sister.

Lily smiles from behind her hair.

Elspeth says, 'Her eyes are blue and dead like a fish.'

'Pay no attention to her,' says the pretty girl. 'I'm Amelia. I'm very pleased to meet you again.' She leans in to air-kiss me on both cheeks and I am almost knocked backwards by the smell of her perfume.

'What do you mean "again"?' I ask.

'We met when we were little. My mum told me. We're the same age.'

'Grandma didn't want you here and neither do we,'

says Elspeth, who I am beginning to suspect doesn't like me.

'Of course we do,' says Freddie.

'What was she like?' I ask, ignoring what Elspeth said.

My cousins exchange glances and, for a moment, I feel like they have some secret way of communicating without speaking.

'She was strong,' says Elspeth at last.

'Strong?' I say, thinking this an odd answer.

'She was sixty-nine,' adds her older sister, Lily. 'But she was still running up and down the stairs in her house every single day.'

'She shouldn't have been,' states Gerald. 'That's how she died. She fell.'

'Her neck was broken,' says Elspeth.

'It's how she would have wanted to go,' says Oberon.

'You think she wanted to fall down the stairs and break her neck?' I say, beginning to understand why Mum wanted to escape from her family. This lot are seriously odd.

'What he means is that she died suddenly and without suffering,' says Amelia. 'She never wanted to suffer.'

The church bells chime and I look over my shoulder to see that Mum is gesturing that it is time to go in.

2

THE FUNERAL

'Devoted wife, attentive mother, doting grandmother and good friend. These are some of the ways in which Flora Considine will be remembered . . .'

The vicar stands in the pulpit, leaning over the lectern. Father Gowlett is quite old with messy white hair and long sideburns that stick out like whiskers. He wears a pair of reading glasses and he keeps adjusting his dog collar as if it is too tight.

'Flora was a rare and valued member of the community and, speaking as one who was privileged to count her as a personal friend, I can say it came as a deep shock to all of us when she was so very suddenly taken from us . . .'

There is no one in the church except my family, the vicar and an old lady sat at an organ. If Grandma was such a valued member of the community, I wonder, how come there are no other friends? Across the aisle I can see

Amelia with her mum and dad. Her mother is elegantly dressed and very beautiful. Amelia's face is wet with tears. I think I can still smell her perfume all the way across the church. In front of her are Freddie and his dad.

'Her beloved husband, Frank, passed away over a decade ago but thankfully Flora was not left alone in the world. All who knew her understood the great consolation she took from her family. Her boys, Harkett, Kitson, Sewell, Robson and William are a constant reminder of her achievements as a mother.'

I glance up at Mum because he has forgotten her. She is wearing the same expression I last saw when we bumped into an old boyfriend of hers with his new wife. She is pretending not to care.

Father Gowlett catches her eye and smiles kindly. 'And although she and her daughter didn't always see eye to eye, I know that Lynda was always on her mind, particularly towards the end of her life.'

I feel something hit the back of my neck. I look behind me. Oberon is tearing off corners of his bible's pages with his teeth and spitting them out. The rest of his family either haven't noticed or are ignoring him.

'But it was when she spoke of her grandchildren that she would truly come alive,' continues Father Gowlett. 'The bond between grandmother and grand-child is often a strong one, and nowhere was this more true than in the Considine family. I hope it will comfort you children, who loved your grandmother so dearly, to remember that her spirit lives on in your hearts and in your prayers.'

I notice he doesn't mention heaven.

'I'd now like to invite Elspeth Considine to give us her tribute to her grandmother.' He smiles and removes his glasses. 'Elspeth is going to read a short poem of her own composition.'

Elspeth walks up to the front and unfurls a piece of paper. She doesn't look the slightest bit nervous or self-conscious.

'Grandma,' she reads. 'Grandma led us with her every step. She breathed life into us with every breath. I wish she were still here to show us the way. She taught us much more than I can say.'

Across the aisle from me, Amelia lets out a sob and her mother puts an arm around her.

'Thank you, Elspeth. That was beautiful,' says Father Gowlett.

Elspeth refolds the poem and returns to her seat.

'Elspeth's lovely verse reminds us that Flora was much more than a grandmother to her grandchildren. She considered herself their spiritual guide. Now that she has passed away, I humbly offer my own services to you children in that capacity. Just as our Lord Jesus Christ is a shepherd to lost sheep, let me be your shepherd. Choosing the right path is difficult when you are young, but if you wish I am always available to help steer you the right way.'

I notice Freddie turn around and look at Amelia, but I can't read his expression from where I am sitting. Mum looks at me and raises an eyebrow. I feel strangely detached from the whole thing.

We sing a couple of hymns, accompanied by the old lady at the organ, who has a small yappy dog that sits in her handbag beside her and barks along with the music. I don't know any of the tunes so I mouth the words from the hymn sheet.

When the sermon is over, we all trudge out through the graveyard and watch as the coffin is lowered into the ground. It is the first coffin I have seen close up and it is smaller than I expected. Father Gowlett says another prayer, then everyone files past the grave to throw handfuls of soil over the top of the coffin. As the ground is frozen, the old lady with the dog holds out a plastic pot filled with earth for us to help ourselves. I grab a handful and throw it on to the coffin lid.

We walk away and Father Gowlett shakes everyone's hands. I watch as he mutters something to each of my cousins. I wonder what he is saying. When it comes to me and Mum, he says, 'Welcome back, Lynda. I'm sorry that we're not meeting under better circumstances.'

Mum is too upset to reply and just nods, but I thank him and we go into the car park.

'So, Lynda, we're having the wake at Louvre House,' says one of my uncles. 'Can you remember the way?'

'I think so. It's been a while though,' replies Mum.

'Perhaps you could give me a lift and I'll direct you,' says Will.

'Oh, thanks,' says Mum, 'that'd be great.'

'Drive carefully,' says Freddie's dad. 'Some of the roads are still pretty icy.'

'Where are you parked?' asks Uncle Will.

'Just a short wade away,' I reply.

'It's not far away,' Mum says.

I lead the way, walking along a bank of snow, trying to avoid the slushy puddles that line the street.

Uncle Will smiles. 'I bet you don't have this kind of problem back home.'

'The snow's new, but Mum's parking is no different,' I reply.

'Watch it, cheeky,' says Mum.

Uncle Will laughs. 'This whole thing must be pretty weird for you, Mariel.'

'Weird's a good word for it,' I reply.

'How were your cousins?' he asks.

'It wasn't the warmest welcome I've ever had,' I say.

'Don't worry. They can be a bit like that with new people. They're very close.'

'I can't wait to meet Madeleine,' says Mum. 'You have to enjoy every moment, while they can't answer you back.'

'I can sit around in diapers and say *goo goo gah* if you want,' I say.

'That wouldn't be quite the same,' replies Mum.

'I don't know, it sounds a lot like Madeleine,' quips Uncle Will.

By the time we get to the turning for Grandma's house, we are laughing. We turn off the main road and drive through an archway towards a large old red-brick building, faded and weathered over the years, but still grand and impressive. It's not the kind of place I imagined Mum growing up in but then I never pictured her with five brothers. We all fall silent as Mum drives slowly up the bumpy driveway, past the leafless trees towards the old house.

'What did you say it was called?' I ask.

'Louvre House. It's been in the family for years,' Uncle Will replies.

The other cars are already parked outside and there are lights on inside the house. Chunky flakes of snow are falling as we step out of the car. The front door to the house is up a couple of stone steps. It has been left open.

'I can't believe you grew up here,' I say, peering into the dark hallway.

'It seems smaller somehow,' says Mum.

'And emptier now she's gone,' adds Uncle Will.

We go into a room full of my uncles and aunts. None of my cousins are there. The wallpaper is torn, the carpet is threadbare and the chandelier that hangs from the ceiling is covered in a thick layer of dust. Beneath it, three of my uncles are talking. Will joins his wife, Chrissie, who is pretty, with strawberry blonde hair and blue eyes. She is sitting on a sofa by the fire holding a sleeping baby. Amelia's mother is getting everyone drinks. I can't remember what she is called. There are so many names to remember.

'Mariel. This is your Uncle Sewell and Aunt Dee.' Mum introduces me to a man wearing black corduroy trousers and his wife, a short-haired woman wearing a red cardigan over a black woollen dress.

'It must be confusing, suddenly having all these new family members out of the blue,' says Uncle Sewell.

'Sewell and Dee are both teachers,' says Mum.

'University lecturers, actually,' corrects Aunt Dee. She has an American accent.

'We live on the university campus. You must come and stay if you have time,' says Uncle Sewell.

'Mariel, have you met our daughters, Lily and Elsepth, yet?' asks Aunt Dee.

'Yes, at the church,' I reply.

'I'm sure they'd love to spend some time with you. I don't know where they could have got to.' She looks around for them.

I am in no hurry to encounter Elspeth again so I say I might get something to eat.

'Good idea. Ruth has excelled herself as usual,' says Aunt Dee.

'Which one's Ruth?' I ask.

'She'll be in the kitchen going for housewife of the year award,' says Aunt Dee.

I follow Amelia's mum through the door that leads to the kitchen. Aunt Ruth is inside taking a tray of sausages out of the oven. She is a short plump lady with her hair cut into a neat bob. She tips the sausages into a bowl.

'You really should stop cooking now,' Amelia's mum says. She has a soft French accent, which makes her seem even more glamorous. 'There's enough to feed an army out there.'

'I'm only warming stuff up, Celeste! Besides, Oberon could happily munch his way through all these sausages himself.'

Aunt Celeste winks at me. 'Why don't you get yourself a drink, Mariel. Have a look in the fridge.'

I find a bottle of lemonade in the fridge and pour myself a glass.

'I think your cousins are upstairs,' says Aunt Ruth. 'I did ask my two to wait for you before they went running off. But boys at that age can be terribly forgetful, can't they?'

'How old are they?' I ask.

'Gerald is seventeen. Oberon is fifteen. They're both very upset. They were very close to Flora.'

'What was she like?' I ask, finding a straw for my lemonade.

Aunt Celeste thinks before replying. 'The word I would use is controlling.'

'Celeste!' scolds Aunt Ruth. 'You shouldn't speak ill of the dead, especially not at the wake.'

'Is that why Mum fell out with her, because she was controlling?'

My two aunts look at one another. 'None of us ever found out why your mother and Flora fell out or why Lynda left like that,' says Aunt Celeste.

'Did she ever mention us?' I ask.

Neither of them answers, then Aunt Ruth says, 'Would you like a sausage before they go through to the ravenous masses?'

'Thank you, no. I don't eat meat,' I say.

'No meat?' says Aunt Ruth. 'Oh well, there's plenty you can eat out there. Would you mind taking these out with you, Mariel?'

I return to the room with the sausages and put them down on the table full of food.

Behind me, three of my uncles are arguing about the house.

'What I'm saying is we should keep it in the family,' says Will.

'You wouldn't really want to move here, would you?' asks another uncle. 'The amount of work needed to make this place inhabitable would be phenomenal.'

'You're seeing it from an architect's point of view,

Harkett,' replies Will. 'If Chrissie and I moved in, it wouldn't need to be perfect.'

'The best thing to do would be to convert it into flats, then sell it,' says Uncle Robson.

'This is our family home, not one of your development opportunities,' says Will.

Freddie's dad holds his hands up defensively. 'I'm just saying there's profit to be made here – for all of us.'

'Some things are more important than profit, Rob,' says Will.

'For what it's worth, I agree with Will,' says Uncle Sewell, joining the discussion. 'I think we should try to keep the house in the family.'

'We're all getting ahead of ourselves anyway,' says Unce Harkett. 'We don't even know what Mum's will says yet.'

3

OBERON'S SWIM

I leave the room to take a look around. Across the hallway is a study with a desk in one corner and piles of
cardboard boxes in the other. There's not much to see
in the other downstairs rooms as their contents are in
large metal trunks. The house is so old and empty it is
difficult to imagine anyone ever living here. I picture
Mum and her five brothers running around the house.
I try to imagine Grandma all on her own here, but I
don't know what she looked like. I decide to go and
look for a picture of her.

The only picture hanging on the wall is a framed
copy of the Mona Lisa, high above the stairs. People
always say she is smiling, but to me her eyes look sad.

At the top of the stairs I stop and listen for any indi-
cation of my cousins but all I can hear is chatter from
downstairs. I open a door into a room with more
trunks inside. There is no carpet in the room and there

19

are wooden shutters instead of curtains. The paint has flaked off the walls and there are wide scratch marks across them. I open one of the trunks up. It is full of ornaments, clothes, plates and things. There are no photos. I try the next room and find the same thing. The next is the bathroom. It's grubby and so cold I can see my breath. Droplets of water drip from a tap on to the discoloured enamel of the bathtub. I twist it and the dripping stops but as I turn my back it starts again.

Stepping into the bedroom at the front of the house I feel carpet beneath my feet. I find a light switch. There is a double bed in the middle of the room and two bedside tables, a wardrobe in the corner and a dressing table by the window. I pick up a framed black-and-white photograph of a young couple on their wedding day. For a moment I think it is Mum and I am confused because she and Dad never got married. Then I realise these are my grandparents. I can see a few similarities between my grandfather and some of my uncles. Freddie has inherited his good looks too. Grandma, though, looks spookily like Mum.

In the photo Grandad is gazing at his new bride while she stares at the camera with a sweet smile on her lips.

I put the photo back and look for another. The top drawer of the dresser is full of jewellery. The drawer below is the same. It seems like an extraordinary amount of jewellery for one person to own. All of it is silver.

In the next drawer I find a pile of loose photos. I take out a handful and leaf through. They are all pictures of my cousins at different ages. There is one of a younger Lily cuddling her baby sister, Elspeth. Another is of Amelia with her hair up and wearing a yellow sash as though she has just won a beauty contest. The only times my uncles and aunts appear in the pictures are when they have been accidentally caught in the background.

I keep flicking through until I come across a picture of my grandmother as she would have looked when she died. It was taken downstairs in the living room. She is sitting on the sofa by the fire, surrounded by her grandchildren. Elspeth sits on one side, Freddie on the other. Amelia is perched prettily on an armchair. Gerald, Lily and Oberon are standing behind the sofa. On Grandma's knee is baby Madeleine. Elspeth is holding a balloon on a string and I wonder whether the picture was taken at Grandma's last birthday. My grandmother's hair is bright white but her eyes are deep brown, just like my cousins'. Her smile reveals unmistakable pride.

Looking at the photo, I feel for the first time since I arrived in this cold country that I have missed out on something. I should have been in the picture. I should have felt the warmth of my grandmother's love. Instead I have lived my whole life without knowing her. I put the photos back.

Turning to leave, I notice a heap of clothes tucked under the bed. It seems odd because the rest of the room has clearly been tidied up after Grandma's death. I lean down to get a better look. A floorboard creaks. I look up and Freddie appears in the doorway.

'Hello there,' he says, grinning. 'Playing hide and seek with yourself?'

'I thought it was traditional at family funerals,' I reply.

Freddie laughs. He walks into the room and spots the pile of clothes. 'Ah, there they are.'

'Are they yours?'

He bends down and gathers them up. 'No, they're Obe's. Look, his shirts are like tents.' He holds one out to demonstrate this.

'Oberon's the large one, the brother of the tall, nervy one, right?'

'Gerald, yes, that's right.'

'And he's taken his clothes off?'

'Yes, he's gone swimming.'

'There's a swimming pool here?'

'Not a pool. It's a lake.'

'But it's snowing.'

'I know. I blame myself. It was me that dared him.'

'He must be freezing.'

'Yeah, I suppose he's got a couple of extra protective layers that the rest of us don't have.' Freddie blows out his cheeks and sticks out his belly. 'Now he's got out and he's freezing cold so I've come to get his clothes.'

'So, you're saying he stripped off here rather than by the lake?'

'It was part of the dare. Silly, I know. Anyway, I'd better get going. We'll all be back in a minute. Oh, and best not mention it to our parents. Thanks.'

He turns and runs down the stairs. He doesn't ask me to join him and I don't feel like inviting myself. Instead I go to the window and look down at the grounds and watch him run full pelt along the path into the trees. If there is a lake outside, it is too dark to see. I wait until all six of them emerge from the woods, dressed in black, looking like six walking shadows as the snow falls around them.

I don't want to look like I have no one to talk to when my cousins come in so I go back to the living room and position myself by baby Madeleine. Babies are useful for this kind of thing because they have no choice about who talks to them. Madeleine's mum, Chrissie, is sweet and I decide that of all my new relatives she and Will are my favourites. She hands me Madeleine. She is as warm as a hot water bottle.

'Hello, Madeleine, I'm your cousin Mariel,' I whisper in her ear.

She gurgles happily in response.

Aunt Chrissie is talking to Aunt Dee about the funeral.

'I still can't believe she wanted it to be held in a

church,' Chrissie is saying. 'When did that woman ever go to church?'

'I think she promised Ben,' says Aunt Dee.

'Who's Ben?' I ask.

'Father Gowlett,' she replies. 'They've known each other for years. Father Gowlett used to visit her every week.'

Madeleine stares unblinkingly into my face. 'She has blue eyes like me.'

'All babies are born with blue eyes,' says Amelia, appearing by my side. She strokes Madeleine's face and makes her smile, causing her eyes to disappear behind her chubby cheeks. 'It can take up to six months so hers will change soon.'

'What makes you think they'll change?' I ask. 'Aunt Chrissie has blue eyes.'

'Madeleine is a Considine. We all have brown eyes,' she replies.

'Except me,' I say.

She smiles in response to this and says, 'I'm sorry we weren't very welcoming at the church.'

'That's OK,' I reply.

The other cousins have gathered around the table of food. Oberon emerges with a plate piled high. His hair is wet and clings to his forehead.

'Did Oberon really just go swimming?' I ask.

Amelia motions me to be quiet and says, 'Yes but Auntie Ruth mustn't find out. She'll only worry.'

Oberon and his mountain of food join us. 'Hello, likkle baby Madsie,' he says, so loudly in her face that she starts to cry. I quickly hand her back to Aunt Chrissie who says she needs a nappy change anyway and takes her out of the room. Oberon doesn't seem to care that he's made his cousin cry. In fact, he looks pleased there is now a spare seat on the sofa for him to sit and eat. He rests the plate on his knees and picks a chicken drumstick off the top.

'Have you tried the chicken, Mariel? It's good,' he says, gnawing into the flesh.

'I'm a vegetarian,' I reply.

Oberon finds this funny.

'Good for you,' says Amelia. 'There are lots of benefits for your skin in not eating meat. I wish I could be so strong.'

'It's not about being strong. I don't like the idea of killing things,' I say.

Oberon snorts. 'We're higher in the food chain. It's our right to eat animals.'

Looking at him shovelling food into his mouth, I think that some of us are higher than others. I decide against saying this.

'It's a shame you're not here for longer,' says Amelia. 'It would be so nice to have a girl my age around.'

I look out of the window at the snow and notice a dark figure staggering through the blizzard towards the house. He holds one hand up to shelter his eyes. In the other he holds something I can't make out but which hangs limply. Whatever it is, he throws it away before he enters the house. I hear the footsteps in the hallway, then Father Gowlett enters.

His hair is even wilder now and decorated with flakes of thick snow.

'Ah, Father, so kind of you to come,' says Aunt Celeste, who is standing by the door. 'Would you care for a drink?'

'No, I can't stay long. None of you can,' he replies. 'The snow is falling heavily. There are warnings on the radio. They are saying it will continue all night. I'm sorry to break up the party but I think you'll be stranded here if you don't leave.'

Uncle Will says, 'It is blowing a bit of a blizzard out there.'

'We should probably get back to the hotel,' says Mum.

'I don't know why you're not just staying with us,' says Aunt Ruth.

'Kitson and I would be happy to have you too,' adds Aunt Celeste.

'That's very kind of you but we didn't want to put anyone out,' says Mum.

'Nonsense, it's not putting anyone out,' says Aunt Ruth. 'The children are all on half-term this week so Mariel will have some youngsters her own age to play with.'

Mum looks at me and says, 'It would be nicer than staying in a soulless hotel room, wouldn't it?'

I want to signal to her that this is a bad idea but I can't think of a way that won't offend all my aunts and uncles. I glance at Oberon who tears off a chewy bit of chicken skin. His pink tongue darts out and he licks his lips.

'You've already paid for the hotel, haven't you?' I say.

'Only the deposit. It wasn't much,' Mum replies.

'Just call and cancel the hotel room,' Uncle Robson says.

'How long did you say you were staying?' asks Uncle Will.

'Ten nights,' says Mum.

'There we are then, two nights with each family.'

'That's a great idea,' says Uncle Sewell. 'That way we all get to properly catch up with you.'

'You can come to ours first as we're nearest,' says Uncle Harkett.

'Well, that would be nice, wouldn't it, Mare?' says Mum.

I don't reply.

'Then it's settled.' Aunt Ruth claps her hands together. Uncle Robson and Mum go into the hall to call the hotel.

Amelia squeals and says, 'It will be such fun!' but my other cousins don't say anything.

'Now all of you must make haste and return home,' says Father Gowlett.

'I think he's right,' agrees Uncle Robson. 'We don't want to get stuck in this old place.'

As everyone is getting ready to leave and saying their goodbyes, I turn around to find Father Gowlett standing behind me.

'This area is not as safe as it seems, Mariel,' he says. 'You must not venture out into the darkness. You understand? You must stay indoors at night.'

I don't know what to say, but he just turns away to leave.

Outside, the night sky is thick with snow. As we drive away from the house, following Uncle Harkett's car, the headlights sweep across the driveway and I see what it was that Father Gowlett threw away before he entered the house. Lying in the snow is a dead rabbit, falling white snow rapidly covering its limp and bloody body.

4

THE BEAST OF WILDERDALE

We follow Uncle Harkett's car on to the main road. The car skids a little as Mum accelerates away and she grips the steering wheel so tightly her knuckles go white. It is the first time we have been alone together since before the funeral.

'I don't want to stay at their house,' I say.

'Whyever not?' she replies.

'My cousins are weird,' I say.

'What does that mean? They all seem fine to me. I mean, everyone's feeling a bit funny today but apart from that . . .'

She doesn't finish her sentence because she is concentrating on the road. She squints to see through the blizzard. She must be having a completely different experience from me if she hasn't noticed how odd my cousins are. My aunts and uncles seem normal enough and I suppose Mum hasn't spent as much time with their children as I have. I decide against telling her about Oberon's clothes and Freddie's story that he went for a swim but I do tell her about Father Gowlett's warning.

'Oh, you don't want to listen to him. He's always been a few hymns short of a sermon. He's probably talking about that silly beast of Wilderdale story.'

'The what?'

'That's what this area is called: Wilderdale. And there's this local myth about a wild animal that roams at night. It's all nonsense of course.'

'What's nonsense is to have flown across the world to bury a woman you haven't spoken to in years and meet a family you've been avoiding since I was a baby,' I say.

'Mare, we've talked about this. We came here to pay our respects.'

'To a woman you cut out of your life?' I say. 'Have we really flown all this way for that?'

'And I wanted to check,' says Mum.

'Check what? That she was dead?'

Mum's silence answers my question.

'You cried when you got the news,' I say.

'I was just relieved that ...' Once again, Mum appears to forget the rest of the sentence. 'Sorry, love, I really do need to concentrate on driving.'

Mum has always got an excuse why we can't talk about the things she doesn't want to talk about.

All my life, whenever I asked why we didn't see or even talk to her mother, Mum would answer that they didn't get on and it was 'best for everyone this way'. Her story was that as she was an 'only child', like me, and since my dad was 'never on the scene', when her own father died she saw no reason for us to remain in England so we moved to Melbourne. I was two years old at the time.

Since then it has always been just the two of us. Mum's boyfriends never last very long and rarely come too close to what she calls 'our compact little family unit'. People say we act more like sisters than mother and daughter. Most of the time, I feel like the older one even though I'm fourteen and she is thirty-seven. But when we argue, she switches back into mother mode. I always know she's about to do it because she uses my full name. The only time she ever mentioned Grandma was if we were in the middle of an argument and I had said something hurtful. She would shout something like, "I knew I should have named you Flora."

For the remainder of the journey I watch the thick snowflakes melt as they hit the windscreen and then get dismissed by the windscreen wiper. I wonder what Grandma could have done that caused her and Mum to fall out so badly.

Uncle Harkett's car turns right, heading up a hill away from the lights of a nearby town. The road takes us through a dark wood into a village with pretty snow-topped cottages that look like something out of a fairytale. A sign on the outskirts of the village welcomes us to Goodling. We follow the car up a gravel driveway, which crunches noisily beneath the wheels.

The snow is coming down heavily and I am covered by the time I reach the front door. Aunt Ruth has already taken off her coat and put her slippers on like she's been there awaiting our arrival all along.

'Come in, welcome, welcome,' she says. 'Shoes on the shoe rack, please.'

I step inside and slip my shoes off.

'Here, let me take your coat, Mariel,' says Aunt Ruth. 'The living room is upstairs.'

'Upstairs?' I say.

'Harkett designed the house himself.'

'The idea was to give us a better view from the living room, where we spend most of our time. And it means there are two floors between our bedroom and that racket teenagers call music these days,' explains Uncle Harkett.

'That was Flora's idea, giving the boys the ground floor,' says Aunt Ruth.

The house is baking hot, causing my cheeks to flush red. We go upstairs and into the spotless kitchen. Gerald is sitting silently on a sofa in the living room.

'Gerald, dear, why don't you make yourself useful and show your cousin where everything is,' says Aunt Ruth.

Gerald looks at me, nods and, without a word, leaves the room. He glances at me on the way out which I think is his way of asking me to follow him. He hasn't spoken to me since we met in the churchyard, but rather than say anything I decide to meet his silence with silence and see how long we can go before one of us speaks. We step on to the top floor and he opens a door to a bathroom. I look inside and nod to indicate that yes, I understand it's a bathroom. He looks at me suspiciously but still says nothing. We go into his parents' bedroom. Like everything else in the house it is meticulously clean and tidy. Again, I silently nod, beginning to enjoy the game. He shows me two spare bedrooms then leads me back down to the ground floor.

He stops outside his bedroom door. 'You should stay away from us.'

'Are you always like this or are you making a special effort because I'm family?' I ask.

He grabs my elbow and grips it tightly. 'If you know what's good for you, you'll leave. You're not a Considine. You're not one of us.'

I try to laugh this off but I don't find it very funny.

'I'm as much your cousin as any of the others. What's wrong with you?'

'Yeah, what's wrong with us, Gerald?' Oberon asks, appearing at the door.

Gerald looks at him fearfully.

'Your brother was warning me to stay away,' I say to Oberon.

A broad grin crosses Oberon's face. 'That's not very nice, bro. Mariel's our cousin. It's nice to have another cousin. It's like finding an extra bit of bacon on your plate.' He laughs at this as though it's the funniest joke in the world.

'I've never been compared to a piece of dead animal before,' I say.

'No, you're a live animal,' replies Oberon, his nostrils flaring. 'Talking of which, I'm hungry.'

Having watched him guzzle down the mountain of food at the wake I find this difficult to believe, but we all go back up to the kitchen where he opens the fridge and starts pulling out food and constructing a huge sandwich.

Gerald watches him nervously. Mum, Uncle Harkett and Aunt Ruth are sitting at the table drinking tea.

I stifle a yawn, not because I'm bored but because exhaustion is catching up with me. My sudden tiredness has a strange effect on me. The lights seem too bright. My eyelids feel heavy. Aunt Ruth shows me to one of the spare rooms upstairs and Mum comes to sit on the bed.

'How are you?' she asks.

'I'm tired,' I say.

'You will try to make an effort, won't you?'

This annoys me but I haven't the energy to start an argument. She kisses me goodnight and leaves.

I close my eyes, then open them and realise I've been asleep. My throat is dry. I check my watch. Two hours have passed. I can't get back to sleep without a drink so I get up and go downstairs in search of a glass of water. My uncle, aunt and mum are chatting in the living room. I slip into the kitchen unnoticed and find a glass.

'Gerald will be going to university in September,' Aunt Ruth is saying.

'Where's he hoping to go?' asks Mum.

'DeCrispin University. The campus is only a couple of miles away from home. Besides, Sewell and Dee can look out for him.'

'Does he need looking out for?' asks Mum.

Aunt Ruth coughs.

Uncle Harkett says, 'He's fine. He's just quiet, always has been. At least Gerald has some intelligence. Oberon is failing everything.'

'He just hasn't found his strengths,' says Aunt Ruth.

'He needs to pull his socks up. I keep telling him but he won't listen. Neither of them will. Flora had more influence over them than either of us.'

'She certainly seemed to have got on with the grand-children more than she ever did with us,' says Mum.

'Oh, she was obsessed with them,' says Uncle Harkett. 'We took the boys away on a two-week summer holiday to France once without her and she didn't speak to us until Christmas. And she was pretty vile to Chrissie until Madeleine finally showed up.'

'They've not been married that long, have they?' says Mum.

'They'd been trying for a baby long before they tied the knot,' replies Uncle Harkett.

'A grandparent loving her grandchildren is completely natural,' says Aunt Ruth.

'Not all of them,' snaps Mum. 'She didn't give two hoots about Mariel.'

I take my glass of water upstairs. I lie in bed wondering why Mum took me away all those years ago. As my mind is weighed down with sleep, the thought grows that she did it because she didn't want to share me with anyone. She wanted me all to herself. She wanted me to grow up under her shadow. My selfish mother, running away from her family so no one could intrude on 'our compact little family unit'.

The next time I wake up it is still dark outside. I check my watch and see that it has just gone three o'clock. I feel strangely awake so I get up and walk to the window. There is a crescent moon in the sky. Fresh white snow on the ground reflects its light, making the scene unusually bright. It has stopped snowing for the moment. Out in the darkness, at the top of a hill, is a tiny orange glow. I wonder what it is. It flickers but it is too far to make out properly.

A movement much nearer catches my eye. Something in the garden. It is too quick to identify. It's pretty big though and I wonder if the foxes are bigger over here. I wonder what other things run around at night in England. In Australia it could have been a possum or a wombat. I think about Father Gowlett's warning.

I go back to bed and find I am able to sleep again, although it is a fitful restless night until daylight finds its way into the room through a slit in the curtains.

5

PERCY'S RUIN

Downstairs, nice morning smells are coming from the kitchen: toast, eggs, coffee. I follow my nose and find Aunt Ruth making breakfast. Mum is sitting at the table with a cup of coffee.

'Morning, darling,' she says.

'Did you sleep well?' asks Aunt Ruth.

'Yes, thanks.'

'Gerald and Oberon haven't surfaced yet. It's always the same during half-term. But teenagers need more sleep than adults, don't they? I read that somewhere. I expect you're the same, Mariel.'

'Mariel's a terrible sleeper, aren't you?'

I know what Mum is about to say and glare at her to try to stop her but as usual she doesn't notice.

'She used to sleepwalk when she was little,' says Mum.

'Mum!' I protest.

'It's all right. Lots of people do it.' Mum laughs. She has told this story a million times before. 'The first time she did it I thought there was a burglar in the house so I called the police, only to find it was Mariel walking around in her pyjamas. Sometimes she would go into the living room and turn on the TV and wake herself up with the noise of it.'

They are both laughing now but I have never found it particularly funny because Mum never mentions how much of a problem it became. She conveniently forgets the time I turned on the cooker and almost burnt the house down or the time I almost jumped out of an upstairs window. She forgets all the experts we went to see and how it made me feel like I wasn't in control of my own body. She forgets all this because a few years ago it stopped happening, but the memory of how it made me feel hasn't gone away.

'And when you woke up did you know why you were there?' asks Aunt Ruth.

'No,' I reply.

'So you weren't dreaming about it as you walked around? I've always thought sleepwalkers must be dreaming about what they're doing.'

'I don't dream,' I say.

Aunt Ruth laughs. 'Everyone dreams.'

'Not me.'

The experts we saw said everyone dreams only not everyone remembers it, but I don't think that's true.

My nights are blanks. For me sleep is black timeless nothingness.

Aunt Ruth says, 'Well, I think my boys would sleep all day if I didn't wake them. I have to lure Oberon out with the smell of breakfast.'

'He's certainly got a healthy appetite,' I say, choosing my words carefully.

'Yes.' Aunt Ruth laughs. 'I sometimes wonder whether he'll become a chef one day, he's got such an interest in food. But he seems more interested in eating it than making it.'

'Perhaps a food critic then,' Mum suggests.

'Perhaps.' Aunt Ruth looks pleased that she is indulging her motherly fantasies then adds, 'Only he's never terribly critical when it comes to food.'

I hear the front door and Uncle Harkett comes up the stairs and into the kitchen holding a carton of milk.

'At last.' Aunt Ruth snatches it off him. 'I was beginning to think you'd had to milk a cow.'

'Mrs McDonnell next door collared me and you know what she's like when she gets talking. It seems another one of her guinea pigs has gone missing.'

'That woman and her guinea pigs. Morning, Oberon.'

Oberon pads into the kitchen, yawning loudly, wearing a stripy dressing gown.

'Smells good. What's cooking?' he says.

'I'm making a traditional English breakfast for our

guests.' She places a plate in front of me piled high with food including three rashers of bacon and two sausages.

'I'm sorry, I don't eat meat,' I say.

'Oh yes, you told me yesterday,' says Aunt Ruth, getting flustered.

'I'll have hers.' Oberon snatches the plate from me. 'M*m*, black pudding,' he says, tucking in.

'What's black pudding?' I ask.

'Congealed pig's blood,' says Oberon, holding up a piece on his fork, then shoving it into his mouth.

'Everything but the bacon, sausages and black pudding would be lovely thank you, Aunt Ruth,' I say.

'You used to love sausages when you were little,' says Mum.

'Apparently I used to love putting my feet into my mouth too. It doesn't mean I want to do it any more,' I reply.

'Oberon, I thought you and Gerald might like to take Mariel for a walk while we're at the reading of the will today,' says Aunt Ruth, as she dishes out a new plate for me.

'You want to go for a walk?' asks Oberon, reaching into his mouth and pulling out a string of bacon rind from between his teeth.

'My shoes are no good in the snow,' I say, not relishing the idea of going out with Oberon.

41

'We can lend you some wellingtons,' says Aunt Ruth.

'Thanks,' I say, although I don't mean it.

'You could take her up to Percy's Ruin,' suggests Uncle Harkett. 'There's a lovely view from there.'

'Percy's Ruin,' says Mum wistfully. 'I can't believe it's still standing.'

'What is it?' I ask.

'It's a folly,' says Uncle Harkett. 'The local authority has been trying to get it pulled down for years but there's a campaign to keep it as a local landmark.'

'What's a folly?' I say.

'Something that was either built foolishly or which has no purpose. Or, as in this case, both. It was built by an ancestor of ours, your great-great-grandfather. You can see it from here.'

'You wanna go after breakfast then?' says Oberon.

There is something unnerving about the way he looks at me. I have no desire to be alone with him but I don't want to appear rude in front of my aunt and uncle so I say yes.

'I'll come with you too,' says Gerald, entering the kitchen.

'Ah, morning, sweetheart. How nice, yes, all three of you can go.'

'Hungry, Gerald?' says Oberon, shovelling a forkful of food into his face.

Gerald doesn't answer but he sits down to eat.

*　　*　　*

42

Before leaving with Uncle Harkett and Mum, Aunt Ruth finds me some hideous purple wellies with yellow flowers. They are a size too big but they do keep my feet dry in the thick snow. Most of the conversation is with Oberon as we trudge up the hill. Gerald walks behind us, as silent as ever. Oberon asks a lot of questions about my life in Melbourne.

'So you go to the beach every day?' he says.

'In the summer, yes.'

'And it was summer there when you left?'

'Yep. Blue skies, hot sun, long days.'

'I like it like this,' he says.

'What, getting dark halfway through the afternoon?' I say.

'I like the dark.' He grins at me. 'There's a good nightlife here, isn't there, Gerald?'

He looks at his brother.

'You mean, like clubs and things?' I remark, finding it hard to believe.

Oberon laughs. 'Not exactly.'

'How far are you planning on taking this?' asks Gerald.

'We're going all the way to Percy's Ruin,' replies Oberon.

I can tell this isn't what Gerald meant. Considering that he's the oldest he does appear to be scared of his brother.

'You want to know why it's called Percy's Ruin?' Oberon asks me, not bothering to wait for an answer.

'Old Percy was Grandad's grandad. He bought the piece of land on top of the hill and built the tower. The problem is the ground is soft around here. Dad says it was crazy to think about building on ground like that. Even while it was being built it started to lean. It cost him loads of money. Then, just after he finished it, a chunk of outside wall fell away. Percy climbed up to the top and threw himself off.'

'He killed himself?'

'That's the story. Poor old Percy.' Oberon smiles.

We have left the village, following a path alongside a field heading towards the woods. The field has a covering of white snow, spoilt only by a few pairs of animal tracks.

Oberon glances over his shoulder at Gerald. 'Let's get him,' he whispers. 'Do what I do.' He scoops up a handful of snow and presses it together. I do the same. 'When I say "now", turn and lob.'

The idea of a real snowball fight is exciting.

'Now!'

He spins round and throws his snowball. It smacks Gerald in the chest. I do the same but mine hits him in the face. Gerald doesn't react. Ice drips down his glasses. He takes them off and wipes them with his scarf.

'Oh, come on, Gerald, retaliate. It's supposed to be fun,' says Oberon.

'This isn't my idea of fun,' he replies.

'Then why did you come?' snaps Oberon.

Gerald doesn't answer and I feel bad as he brushes the ice off his scarf.

It's darker in the woods, even though most of the trees are bare and leafless. Oberon pulls out a chocolate bar from his pocket. He takes a bite and then, as a second thought, offers it to me. I don't fancy the end he thrusts in my direction because it has his toothmarks and glistens with saliva.

We reach a clearing at the top of the hill where the tower stands. Percy's Ruin is impressive up close. It stands at the top of the hill, looming high above the nearest trees. I can understand why Percy wanted to build it there. The view is amazing.

'That's our house,' says Oberon, pointing it out. 'That's the university where Lily and Elspeth live. That's the old pea factory where Freddie lives. And that's Amelia's cottage down there. You can see Percy's Ruin from most the houses around here.'

I look up at the tower and notice that the top is blackened by smoke. I realise that this is where I saw the light last night. The spiral staircase that runs through its centre is visible where a section of wall halfway up has fallen away. It reminds me of those drawings you get of buildings which are designed to show you the inside and out. A wire fence surrounds the base of the tower with signs that read *DANGER: DO NOT ENTER. UNSAFE STRUCTURE.*

'You want to go up it?' asks Oberon.

'Not really,' I reply. 'Going up a wonky tower with half a wall missing isn't exactly my idea of fun.'

'Oh, come on,' says Oberon. 'It's an even better view from the top. You can see the whole of Chilton.'

He pushes the wire fence down and easily steps over it. I follow him in and approach the tower. 'It's completely safe,' he says. 'I've done it loads of times.' He goes through the open doorway and up the stairs. I peer inside the tower. It is dark and damp. I don't want to say it but the prospect of going up with someone as heavy as Oberon makes the idea even less appealing.

'I'll wait here and wave at you,' I suggest.

'You're not a coward like my brother, are you, Mariel?' he asks.

'She said she didn't want to go.' Gerald is standing next to me at the entrance to the tower.

Oberon comes back down. The intensity of his stare frightens me. 'Stay out of this, bro,' he growls. 'We've all done it. Even him.' He points at Gerald. 'It's not really dangerous. You'd have to be an idiot to fall and you're not an idiot are you, Mariel?'

Gerald pushes in front of me and squares up to his brother. 'I know what you're doing.'

'Of course you do,' says Oberon. 'After all, Gerald is the brains of the family, aren't you? You're the one who's never in trouble.'

'Trouble? Is that what you call it?'

'Look, no one's getting in trouble,' I say, 'because I'm not going up.'

'Suit yourself,' says Oberon and he storms out of the tower. He pushes Gerald out of the way and runs down into the woods.

I turn to Gerald for some kind of explanation but he avoids my gaze as usual.

'What's wrong with you people?' I ask.

'You shouldn't be here,' he says, then silently leads me back down in the direction of the house.

6

HER BELOVED GRANDCHILDREN

When we get back to the house, Oberon is sitting in the living room with his parents and my mum.

'Gerald, Mariel, sit down please,' says Aunt Ruth. 'We have something to tell you.'

'This doesn't concern her,' says Oberon.

'Oberon, don't be so rude,' scolds Aunt Ruth.

'Flora left it to *all* her grandchildren. That includes Mariel,' says Mum.

'To her "*beloved* grandchildren",' snaps Oberon. 'Grandma didn't mean her.'

'What are you talking about?' asks Gerald.

'The will,' says Uncle Harkett. 'Your grandmother split her money evenly between her children, but she left the house to you and your cousins.'

'To us?' says Gerald.

'Yeah,' says Oberon. 'Her *beloved* grandchildren.'

'Which includes Mariel,' says Mum.

Oberon storms out, slamming the door behind him. My uncle and aunt look apologetically at Mum.

'He is taking your mother's death pretty hard,' says Aunt Ruth. 'She was like a mentor to him.'

Under her breath Mum mutters, 'Poor him,' but no one else hears her and the conversation moves on to what should be done with the house.

'The most sensible thing to do is to sell it and split the proceeds eight ways,' says Uncle Harkett. 'The question is whether to sell it as it is or do it up first and get a better price.'

'I can't help feeling sorry for Will,' says Mum. 'He and Chrissie were hoping they would be able to move in.'

Gerald remains silent. I don't say anything either, because I don't really want to own even a percentage of a spooky old house and, if I'm honest, I agree with Oberon. Grandma probably didn't mean me when she said "beloved grandchildren".

More snow falls in the afternoon. I watch TV with Gerald but he shows no interest in talking to me.

The parents sit chatting and drinking tea until Uncle Harkett decides it is time to open a bottle of wine. Oberon emerges for dinner but doesn't say much, then goes back to his room.

I can tell Mum is enjoying herself, reminiscing with Uncle Harkett. She keeps laughing loudly and trying to involve me in the stories, but I feel distant from her so I pretend to be interested in the TV until it is late enough to go to bed.

In the middle of the night I wake with a jolt. It is dark. I can hear a noise. It sounds like a rattling door but the sound keeps stopping and starting and I can't get to sleep for the anticipation of the next time I will hear it. Frustrated, tired and groggy, I get up and go to see if I can stop it.

It isn't any of the doors on the floor below so I go down to the ground floor where my cousins sleep. It is Oberon's door that is rattling. I grip the handle and hold it in place to stop it, but I can't stand there all night like this, so I push the door open. It creaks and I freeze for fear of disturbing Oberon. There is no movement so I push it further and see that Oberon's window is open. His curtain is flapping in the wind and soft moonlight spills into the room. The only choice I have is to close the window. If Oberon can sleep through the rattling door, he can sleep through anything. I step inside and look at his bed. It is empty.

I pull the window shut and leave the room, closing the door behind me. I run upstairs and climb back into bed. Where is Oberon? My imagination runs wild until I hear a toilet flush and I realise that he probably just got up to go to the loo. I begin to wonder whether this place is making me go insane.

* * *

In the morning neither Oberon nor Gerald are awake to say goodbye, which I am relieved about. I persuade Aunt Ruth not to bother waking them. We are staying with Kitson and Celeste next. Amelia was nice to me at the funeral so I hope our stay with her is a bit more normal.

We leave the hire car at Uncle Harkett's and he takes us in his car because there is still snow on the roads and his car has four-wheel drive.

Kitson and Celeste live in Todminton on the other side of the hill, right below Percy's Ruin. We pull up outside a quaint white-walled cottage with a thatched roof.

The door to the cottage opens and Amelia and her mum come out. They both look like they have just stepped out of a stylish winter clothes catalogue. I feel self-conscious in the purple wellies Aunt Ruth gave me.

We get out of the car and Celeste kisses Mum on both cheeks. Mum isn't prepared for this and only narrowly avoids a head collision. Amelia greets me in the same way and says, 'I'm so glad you're staying. We're going to have such fun.' Her perfume is overpowering.

'Kitson's out on a housecall,' Aunt Celeste says.

'Is he a doctor?' I ask.

'Dad's a vet,' says Amelia.

Uncle Harkett gets back into his car. 'We'll see you at Robson's get-together,' he says.

The rest of us go into the cottage and sit on stools at a breakfast bar in the kitchen. The cottage is colourfully decorated with vases of fresh bright flowers and bowls of potpourri everywhere. Aunt Celeste makes coffee for Mum and freshly squeezed orange juice for me.

'Amelia has an audition this afternoon in Chilton,' Aunt Celeste says. 'We thought you might like to get the train in with us and go shopping.'

'Audition for what?' I ask.

'I'm up for a part in an advert,' says Amelia. 'I've been modelling mostly so far but I go for acting jobs when I can. After all, acting is just modelling with speaking really. You can help me pick out what to wear for the audition.'

'What's the part?' asks Mum.

'It's for a fabric softener. In the advert I put on a jumper, notice the smell and then say, "Wow, that's fresh."'

'Now, darling, remember the emphasis,' says Aunt Celeste. '"Wow" and "fresh" are the important words.'

'W*ow*, that's *fresh*,' says Amelia again.

I try it too. Then mum has a go. Soon we are all trying to find different ways to say it and laughing. Each time someone says it the sentence becomes funnier. By the time Uncle Kitson comes home we are falling about laughing.

'Hello, Daddy.' Amelia kisses him on the cheek.

Aunt Celeste pours him a coffee. 'How was your morning?' she asks.

'There's been another one of those attacks. Old Mr Clyde's dog this time.'

'What attacks?' ask Mum.

'Some of the local pets have been attacked at night. Mr Clyde's Alsatian, Molly, is no softy either. She can look after herself normally, but she's scared of her own shadow now. Whatever it was, it shook her up all right.'

'Will she be OK?' asks Amelia.

'Her leg will heal, but her spirit will take longer to return.'

'You think there's something out there attacking pets?' I ask him.

'Molly didn't do it to herself. Some people say there's an animal out there in the woods,' says Uncle Kitson.

'The beast of Wilderdale,' says Aunt Celeste, putting on a spooky voice.

'They've been saying that for years. I remember Dad telling me never to go into the woods. It's just local folklore,' Mum says.

'Well, the beast of Wilderdale may be a myth, but something attacked Molly.'

Amelia and I go to her room. She has a lot of clothes so I sit on her bed and watch as she pulls out various outfits. She disappears behind a screen to change each time but keeps talking to me about the audition and how she should say the line and how pleased she is that I am here.

'Would you mind getting my necklace with the green leaf from the dressing table? I think it will go well with this dress,' she says.

I can't see anything on top of the dresser for all the bottles of perfume.

'Where is it?'

'It's there somewhere,' she replies.

I open a drawer. It is full of silver jewellery, just like the one in Grandma's bedroom.

'It might be hanging from the mirror,' she says.

I look up and see the necklace. I shut the drawer and hand the necklace to her. Amelia emerges wearing a bright pink puffy dress. 'It's too much, isn't it? You don't have to be kind. I'd rather you were honest. What do you think?'

'Maybe something a bit more casual would be better,' I say.

Amelia nods and vanishes behind the screen again.

In the end when we leave for town she is wearing a pair of jeans and a red top.

'I'm surprised trains are still running with all this snow,' says Mum.

'Me too,' says Aunt Celeste, 'but I checked this morning and by some miracle there are still trains today. Everyone moans about the snow in this country but to me it is very beautiful.'

'You and Kitson were still living in France when I emigrated,' says Mum. 'Weren't you tempted to stay there?'

'Oh yes, I would have happily stayed in France but there was no question of it. Flora made that clear when we came over for your father's funeral. How you managed to get away, Lynda, I don't know. Your mother used Frank's death to make all her sons come home. She made them feel guilty until they all gave in and came back.'

'Grandma just wanted her family around her,' says Amelia defensively.

Todminton station is little more than an empty platform and a closed ticket office. Aunt Celeste and Mum sit inside a shelter to wait for the train. Amelia and I walk along the platform together.

'Why did Grandma want everyone close by?' I ask.

'She always taught us to look after each other,' replies Amelia.

'Like how you all looked out for Oberon when he went swimming in the lake the other day?'

'Like that, yes,' replies Amelia.

'I don't think he likes me,' I say.

'Oh, take no notice of him. You know what boys are like,' says Amelia dismissively.

I'm tempted to tell her about the open window in his room last night, but instead I ask, 'What will you all do with Louvre House?'

'It's yours too,' says Amelia. 'She left it to all of us.'

'Try telling Oberon that,' I say.

'You really shouldn't worry about him. He's just very upset about Grandma dying.'

'So everyone keeps saying.'

7

AMELIA'S AROMA

The houses on the outskirts of Chilton are big and spaced out with well-kept gardens but the ones closer to the town centre stand shoulder to shoulder and have small concrete yards at the back. The train crosses an icy canal and enters the station. Aunt Celeste and Amelia point us in the direction of their favourite shops and we arrange to meet up in a cafe after Amelia's audition.

'Good luck with the audition,' I say.

'You're supposed to say "Break a leg" when it's acting,' Amelia replies.

I feel like saying that putting on a jumper and saying three words is barely acting but Amelia has been nothing but nice to me so I reply, 'Break a leg.'

Mum lets me buy what I want and doesn't seem to mind how much it all costs.

'What are credit cards for?' she says breezily.

For Mum, shopping solves lots of problems. She takes me shopping if we've had an argument and she wants to make up. Or if she has split up with a boyfriend and wants to make herself feel better. Or if she's just feeling down and in need of some 'retail therapy'. Today she is feeling guilty. As we step outside the shopping centre she says, 'I really am sorry I didn't tell you about my family all this time.'

'Sorry?' I snap. 'You keep my entire family secret from me all my life and you think one shopping trip will make it all better. You've lied to me my whole life.'

'I've always acted with your best interests at heart.'

'What? Being kept away from my family? Never knowing my cousins?'

'You don't know what that woman was like,' she says.

'You mean my grandma?' I say. 'What was wrong with her? She seemed to get on well enough with everyone else.'

'There are things you don't understand,' replies Mum quietly. 'We've had a nice morning. Don't let's spoil it with an argument. Look, there's Father Gowlett.'

The wild-haired vicar is coming out of a shop. She waves and gets his attention and he comes over to join us. He has a long cardboard box tucked under his arm.

'How are you coping, Lynda?' he asks. 'The death of a parent is always hard, no matter how well you got on in life . . . and Flora's death was such a terrible shock to us all. It took me back to . . . well . . .'

He drifts off and Mum says, 'We all have to go one way or another,' which I think sounds a bit heartless.

'You should come to my service on Sunday. I'll be saying a prayer for Flora again.'

'Maybe we will,' says Mum, although I can tell by the way she says it she has no intention of going. She has never been interested in religion.

Father Gowlett turns to me. 'And Mariel, how are you getting on with your cousins?'

'OK,' I say.

I am intrigued by what he has tucked under his arm. 'What is that?' I ask.

Father Gowlett smiles and says, 'This? It's my rifle. One of my little vices, I'm afraid.'

'You shoot animals?' I ask.

'Oh no, I can't shoot any of God's creations. The pigeons in my sights are all very much of the clay variety. And there's something about looking up to the heavens and really concentrating that almost feels like praying sometimes. It's most relaxing.'

He and Mum talk about Grandma leaving the house to the grandchildren, to which he replies, 'She did love those children.'

*   *   *

The cafe is called *Le Parisien*. It has a mural of Paris on the walls and French music playing. Mum and I arrive first and a hassled waitress with a ribbon in her hair shows us to a table and takes our order.

At the table next to us a sweet old couple sit drinking tea. It makes me think of my grandparents. I had no choice about meeting Grandad but I could have known my grandmother if Mum hadn't decided to keep us apart. I wonder once again how she could have kept everything secret from me.

Amelia and Aunt Celeste arrive. Mum waves at them and they join us at the table. As they approach I notice Amelia looks upset and her make-up is smudged around the eyes where she has been crying.

Mum obviously hasn't noticed these details because she cheerfully asks, 'So, how did it go?'

'They said I stank,' Amelia replies miserably.

'They did not say that,' says Aunt Celeste.

'That's what they meant.'

'It wasn't about you. It's your condition.' Aunt Celeste strokes her hair. 'And they can't make a decision based on that. It's discrimination.'

'What condition?' I ask.

'It's a genetic fault that affects her liver enzyme,' says Aunt Celeste.

Mum asks, 'What does that mean?'

'It means I smell.' Amelia bursts into tears.

I realise that a stench that appeared when they

entered isn't coming from outside. It is coming from her. The smell of perfume that normally surrounds her has gone. In its place is something terrible. I'm not the only one to notice it either. People on other tables are turning up their noses in disgust and whispering about us.

'My poor girl,' says Aunt Celeste, putting a comforting arm around her shoulder.

'It's not fair,' sobs Amelia. 'How could they even consider me for an advert for fabric conditioner when I smell like something that lives in a sewer.'

'You do not. Now, why don't you go and use the bathroom to freshen up?' whispers Aunt Celeste in her ear. She pulls out a bottle of perfume from her handbag and hands it to Amelia. Amelia takes it and crosses the cafe to the toilet as quickly as she can manage.

'It's a genetic condition,' says Aunt Celeste quietly.

'So it's hereditary?' says Mum.

'Apparently so,' says Aunt Celeste. 'The specialist called it a recessive gene but neither Kitson nor I have ever come across it before. It's so unfortunate for her.'

'And there's nothing you can do?' says Mum.

'Mostly it's possible to keep it under control with scented oils and perfumes but when she gets agitated it gets worse and they kept us waiting for so long today. Amelia didn't want to keep going to freshen up in case she missed her call.'

Amelia comes out of the toilet and Aunt Celeste

changes the subject. 'Well, I can see you two had a good shopping trip.'

'What did you get?' asks Amelia. 'I wish I could have come with you.' She has reapplied her make-up and doused herself in perfume and speaks brightly like nothing has happened.

'I got some boots a bit like yours,' I show them to her.

'You should put them on now. You must be so tired of wearing those awful wellies.'

The waitress comes over with mine and Mum's order. Aunt Celeste orders cake. Amelia seems back to normal and no one mentions the audition again.

It's fun spending time with Amelia. She seems so confident and sure of herself apart from the outburst in the cafe. Being with her is a million times more enjoyable than spending time with Oberon and Gerald. I like Aunt Celeste too, even when she tries to give me chicken for dinner, on the basis that chickens are really only vegetables with wings.

It gets late and Amelia shows me the room I'll be sleeping in. It's full of flowers. I realise now the flowers and potpourri are there to help mask the smell.

My third night in England passes without incident. I fall straight to sleep and do not wake in the night. As usual my sleep is free from dreams and I awake refreshed for the first time since I landed in this cold country.

8

THE SLAUGHTERED COW

I spend the following day with Amelia, chatting and watching TV. Aunt Celeste apologises because she thinks she should be showing us the sights but Mum and I are happy to relax. In the afternoon Amelia shows me an album of photos of her, including some modelling ones in which she is wearing heavy make-up and pouting at the camera.

'This is my favourite,' she says of one of them. 'Uncle Will took it. He's an excellent portrait photographer but he prefers to do arty photographs, only there's no money in those. That's what Dad says. What I love about photography is that it can really capture a moment. I'm definitely going to concentrate on modelling not acting from now on. One agent told me I have professional cheekbones.'

'Better than amateur ones,' I reply.

She laughs. It's the first time she has come close to

referring to the audition yesterday. I turn the page and see a photograph taken at a wedding.

'This was taken when Uncle Will and Aunt Chrissie got married,' she says.

'How long ago was it?' I ask. 'You all look really young.'

'About four years ago. I was ten I think. So Elspeth must have been four and Lily must have been the same age Elspeth is now. We were all bridesmaids.'

In the photo Amelia, Lily and Elspeth are wearing identical pink dresses, holding tiny bunches of flowers.

'Elspeth doesn't look very happy,' I say. Even as a little girl, dressed in a puffy pink dress, there is a dark brooding look in her eyes.

Amelia laughs. 'She's not a natural bridesmaid. Lily looks pretty though, doesn't she? I always tell her she should wear her hair back.'

In the photo Lily has had her hair in a ribbon. Amelia's right. She has a pretty face but it seems to me that she has lifted the bunch of flowers up to try to hide behind them. Only Amelia looks completely comfortable in front of the camera.

'You're going to theirs next,' says Amelia. 'Mum said Uncle Sewell is coming to take you to the campus tomorrow morning. It's such a shame you couldn't stay longer with me. School holidays can be lonely.'

'Won't you see any friends?' I ask.

Amelia closes the photo album and puts it away. For

a moment I wonder whether she heard my question but I can tell she did. She just doesn't want to answer. It's an awkward moment and we are both grateful when Aunt Celeste calls us for dinner.

When we go down, Uncle Kitson and Mum are already sitting at the table.

'The whole business is bizarre,' Uncle Kitson is saying.

'What business?' asks Amelia.

'I got a call from Farmer Dooley this morning. One of his cows was attacked in the night.'

'Attacked?' I say.

Uncle Kitson nods. 'Attacked and killed,' he says.

'What by?' I ask.

'Well, that's the odd thing. Dooley claims to have seen Oberon running out of the shed.'

Amelia laughs. 'That's ridiculous. Everyone knows Farmer Dooley is as mad as a badger.'

'Yes, last month he was in the paper claiming his chickens were being killed by the beast of Wilderdale,' says Aunt Celeste.

'That was just foxes,' says Uncle Kitson.

'So is that what attacked the cow?' I ask.

'A fox couldn't have done that kind of damage,' says Uncle Kitson.

'I suppose something could have escaped from a zoo,' says Mum.

'It must have been pretty strong to do that to a cow,'

says Uncle Kitson. 'Half the flesh was ripped off its carcass and the poor thing's throat was torn out.'

'That's enough now.' Aunt Celeste carries a pot with a pair of oven gloves and places it on the table. 'We don't want that sort of talk at the table.'

The conversation moves on but I can't stop thinking about what Uncle Kitson said. Aunt Celeste has made beef stew for everyone and ratatouille for me. The beef in the stew is obviously quite tough and I am put off my food by the way they all have to chew so much. I can't help imagining they are eating the same poor cow with its throat torn out. If I had dreams, it would probably form the basis for a nightmare.

Perhaps it is because I go to bed hungry that I awake in the middle of the night.

I am standing up.

Sleepwalking is something you never get used to and it has been a long time since I last walked in my sleep. It takes me a moment to realise I am standing in Amelia's bedroom. Her bed is empty. Outside a security light goes off and makes me jump. I go to the window and look through a gap in the curtain. It is too dark to see much but I can make out Percy's Ruin. Just like before there is a fire at the top of it. I can see the flames flickering. I stand for a moment transfixed, listening to the sounds of the house, watching as the smoke from the fire drifts and twists in the breeze.

I check the bathroom for Amelia but it is empty. I search for her in the living room and the kitchen. She isn't there either. I feel sure that wherever she is, she is no longer in the house.

I go back to the window and look up at Percy's Ruin. I think about the dead cow and the idea of Oberon running from the farmer's shed. I think about my cousins returning after Oberon's swim at Louvre House. I don't know what to make of any of it but there is no way I can go back to sleep so I get dressed. Something inside me urges me to go out and find Amelia. I remember Father Gowlett's warning to stay inside. Terror spreads through my body as I put on my new boots but something drives me on. A key is in the lock. I take it, put on my coat and step outside.

It is cold and dark. I must be mad to have left the house but still I don't go back. Instead I find a large stick to defend myself with and walk up the driveway, across the road, up towards Percy's Ruin. The most direct route is through the woods, up the hill. It is difficult to see where I am going and I instantly wish I had a torch. All I have by way of light is the soft glow of the half moon.

My progress is slow. Walking in the dark is difficult enough. The icy surface and deep snow make it even more so. I stumble and trip but I use my stick for balance. It's bitterly cold. A sharp wind cuts through my clothing and makes me shiver. I think longingly about my bed.

Something howls. It sounds like a dingo I heard once on a school trip but there are no dingoes in England. Whatever is making the noise, it is close by. I feel scared and vulnerable. My stick, which had felt like a proper weapon when I picked it up, now feels flimsy and inadequate. The howling stops but this only makes me more scared. I don't feel safe on the ground so I drop the stick and find a tree to climb. I've always been a good tree-climber but the ice which coats its branches makes it difficult and a couple of times I slip and bang my elbows and graze my chin on the way up.

The trees cast strange shadows on the snowy ground. A papery cloud covers the moon and the shadows vanish. There is something down there. I strain to see what it is. Two red eyes stare out from under the thicket. It is too dark to see what they belong to but I know it's looking at me. I can hear it breathing. I think about the stories about the beast of Wilderdale. Why have I come out at night? What is wrong with me? My body goes rigid and I pray that the creature can't climb trees.

Eventually the animal continues down the hill. My heart is beating fast but I would die of cold if I stayed in the tree all night and I feel like the danger has passed so I climb back down.

Perhaps it's because the animal headed down the hill, but I decide to finish what I have started and pick up the stick. I carry on up the hill to Percy's Ruin moving as quickly as I can. The woods are filled with strange sounds, but I don't hear the howling again. The half moon reappears from behind a cloud, making it easier to see.

I reach the top of the hill where the tower stands. The fire has almost burnt out. Something on the ground glints in the moonlight. I bend down and pick it up. It's a silver crucifix. I hold it up and examine it. It's badly scratched but there is something pleasing about the way it catches the moonlight when I wipe off the dirt. I put it in my pocket and head back down the hill, holding my stick out, ready to hit anything that attacks me.

I am relieved to reach the cottage and let myself in. I replace the keys and tiptoe back to my room. As I pass Amelia's bedroom I notice that the door is shut.

9

MONA LISA'S SMILE

The sound of the howling stays with me. In a story bloodcurdling howls and tales of viciously attacked animals would mean werewolves, but this is real life and I don't believe in anything supernatural. Ask me, if it can't be understood by science it's just because no one clever enough has come along to explain it yet. Besides, werewolves only change when there is a full moon and last night's moon still had a dark shadow across half of it. I laugh at myself for even thinking it.

There was a time when I would have told Mum about what happened last night but since we landed in this cold country it is like we have frozen apart from one another.

Amelia is the last to appear at the breakfast bar and, from the aroma that follows her into the room, I can tell she has applied her usual collection of perfumes.

'Did you sleep well, darling?' asks Aunt Celeste.

'Like a log,' she replies.

'I think left to her own devices my girl would sleep her whole life away,' says Aunt Celeste, kissing her on the forehead.

'I might go back to bed now. I'm feeling rather tired,' Amelia jokes.

'I woke up in the middle of the night,' I say, watching Amelia for a reaction. 'I couldn't sleep.'

She just says, 'It's so annoying when that happens,' and pours herself a bowl of cereal.

Uncle Sewell arrives to take us to his house. Aunt Celeste and Amelia air-kiss us goodbye. Lily and Elspeth are sitting on the back seat. Lily is on the far side, hiding behind her curtain of black hair. Elspeth is sitting nearest. She looks at me coldly when Uncle Sewell opens the back door for me.

'Come on now, Elspeth, move up, make room for your cousin,' says Uncle Sewell.

She unclips her seat belt and moves into the middle seat.

I take my place next to her. Mum sits in the front. Uncle Sewell starts the car. I turn to wave at Amelia but the front door is already shut. Neither Lily nor Elspeth speak, but Elspeth catches my glance every time I look at her, as though daring me to say something.

'I've got to go to Louvre House before I take you to the campus,' says Uncle Sewell. 'There are some documents I need to find. Besides, we all left in a bit of a hurry the other day. Dee wants me to check that all the food is cleared away and that everything is locked up. If it's going to stay empty for a while, we don't want to attract unwanted creatures, do we?'

'What kind of unwanted creatures?' I ask.

'Oh, you know, tigers, panthers, that kind of thing,' says Uncle Sewell.

Uncle Sewell and Mum laugh.

'I mean rats or mice,' he says. 'Although, the name Louvre House suggests the site may have been a home to bigger pests once.'

'I always thought it had something to do with the art gallery in France,' says Mum. 'Isn't that why Dad put up that picture of the Mona Lisa?'

'Louvre is certainly French,' says Uncle Sewell. 'It comes from the words *loup* meaning wolf and *vivre* meaning live. So, literally it means where the wolves live.' The way he says it, it isn't difficult to imagine him delivering a lecture at the university.

'Wolves?' says Mum.

'There was probably some kind of wolf den before it was cleared out and built on,' explains Uncle Sewell. That was back when there were still wolves in this country.

Elspeth leans over and whispers in my ear, 'I know where the wolves run, I know where they hide. You'll know when they strike, but only I where they reside.'

She says it quickly and with a menacing tone and I don't know how to respond but my mind is racing.

Wolves. I think about the howling from last night. I remember the red eyes and suddenly feel certain that they saw me as clearly as I saw them.

Uncle Sewell and Mum are talking about something to do with the tax on Grandma's house.

'Do you want to hear another poem?' asks Elspeth.

I really don't but Elspeth isn't giving me a choice. She looks me in the eyes and recites another. 'My own fear chokes my throat, like I'm swallowing something wrong, but your fear tastes different, it's sweet upon my tongue.'

'That's delightful,' I say. 'How about you, Lily – do you write poetry too?'

'No,' she replies.

'How about you, Mariel?' mimics Elspeth. 'Do you write poetry too?'

'Sometimes,' I reply.

'I bet it's rubbish,' she says.

'Elspeth! Mariel's our cousin,' scolds Lily.

'What are you lot talking about back there?' asks Uncle Sewell, glancing in the rear-view mirror.

'Nothing much,' replies Elspeth.

'Plotting and scheming, no doubt,' he says, smiling.

'We never plot or scheme,' says Elspeth. She leans over and whispers to me. 'Grandma hated you and your mother.'

'What's that, darling?' asks Uncle Sewell.

'Nothing, Daddy,' she answers out loud.

*   *   *

The snow hasn't been cleared beyond the stone arch by the entrance to the grounds. Uncle Sewell stops the car so we can walk up the driveway to the house. As soon as we're out of the car Elspeth asks him for the keys then runs on ahead.

'Be careful you don't slip,' warns Uncle Sewell. He turns to Mum. 'They have so much energy at that age, it's exhausting watching them.'

Lily and I walk behind Uncle Sewell and Mum.

'I'm sorry,' she says quietly. She avoids eye contact.

'Why are you sorry?'

'Elspeth doesn't mean to be like that. She's young.'

'She doesn't seem that young.'

'That's because she spends all her time with her cousins and we're all older than her.'

'Doesn't she have any friends?' I ask.

'No.'

I turn to Lily but she is hiding behind her hair. Ahead, Elspeth has reached the house and let herself in.

'Why did she call me a half-cousin when we first met?' I ask.

'She's just being childish. But you shouldn't want to be one of us. You should do what Gerald told you to do and keep away from us.'

'How do you know what he told me?'

'We spoke on the phone.'

'You're all very close,' I say.

'We only have each other. We don't have friends.'

'Why not?'

Lily falls silent.

'What's wrong with you all?' I ask.

'We have ...' She pauses for such a long time, I wonder whether she is going to finish her sentence at all. 'We have problems.'

'What problems?' I am beginning to suspect that all my cousins are mad.

She doesn't answer. We are getting near the house. Elspeth appears at an upstairs window. She opens it and shouts, 'Lily, come up here.'

'Be careful, Elspeth,' yells Uncle Sewell.

'I'm being careful, Daddy,' she replies. 'Come on, Lily, let's play our game.'

'I'd better go,' says Lily apologetically.

She runs into the house. Uncle Sewell turns to me. 'Too much energy for you as well, eh?' he says, smiling.

'That's the thing about teenagers,' says Mum. 'It's like the energy they had a few years ago gets drowned in all those hormones.'

But it isn't lack of energy that stopped me running in. It was the lack of an invite. Once inside the house, Mum and Uncle Sewell go into the messy study to look for the documents.

Alone in the hallway, I look up at the picture of the Mona Lisa. Today she looks like someone trying hard to smile but failing. I climb the stairs. I can hear Lily and Elspeth moving around in one of the rooms. I realise that, without thinking about it, I am trying to walk without making any noise, not because I'm trying to sneak up on my cousins but because I don't want Elspeth to find me there. I stop on the top stair where I can hear the two of them talking quietly in one of the rooms.

'We have to find it and destroy it,' says Elspeth.

'But we've looked everywhere. It's not here.'

'We can't have looked everywhere or else we'd have found it by now.'

There is a flicker of movement through the slit between the door and the wall. I don't want to be caught eavesdropping so I move quickly into another room full of large metal trunks. I open one. The lid is heavy and the metal is cold. Inside are old musty clothes. I can no longer hear Elspeth and Lily's voices.

Perhaps all families are this bizarre when you look at them up close. It just takes an outsider like me to show it.

'Get your hands off our stuff.'

I turn around. Elspeth is standing behind me.

'Why are you so unpleasant all the time?' I say.

She laughs. 'Grandma didn't love you. You shouldn't be here. This is Grandma's stuff and she left it all to us, not you.' Elspeth pushes the lid shut on the trunk I have opened.

'What is your problem?' I ask.

'You. You don't belong in this family. We don't want you,' she replies.

'You mean you don't. Amelia was nice to me,' I say.

'Amelia's only other company is her own smell.'

'You're a vile little girl.'

I leave the room and walk down the stairs but I stop halfway and turn around, angry that I have given in. Mona Lisa looks down at me and I feel like now she is smiling to hide her anger. Sunlight spills in through a side window. The picture frame casts an uneven shadow, revealing that the picture isn't flat against the wall. I try to get a closer look but it's too high to reach.

There is an umbrella by the door. I run down and grab it. I can hear Mum and Uncle Sewell talking in the study. Using the umbrella as a lever to move the picture I cause something to fall. I step back and narrowly avoid falling down the stairs. I grab the banister to steady myself. A small black book is on the stair. It has scuffed edges and it is held shut by a threadbare piece of string. I tuck it into the back of my jeans. I look up at the Mona Lisa. *That's why she was smiling*, I think, *she had something to hide.*

10

A HONEYBEE FAMILY

The car journey back from Louvre House is made uncomfortable by the book tucked into my jeans and unpleasant by Elspeth whispering insults, unheard by Uncle Sewell and Mum, and ignored by Lily. I shouldn't feel intimidated by this weird little girl but there is something unnerving about her.

The university campus isn't what I expect. I saw a film set in a British university once and it was all lovely old buildings and students whizzing about on bicycles but DeCrispin University is modern and grubby-looking. There isn't a bicycle in sight and the students are dressed in ordinary scruffy clothes rather than the black robes I saw in the film.

Uncle Sewell parks the car and I wait for Elspeth to leave first because I need to secure the book before I get out.

'Can't be many children your own age around on campus,' Mum is saying to Elspeth and Lily.

'That's true, but there's a massive library,' replies Elspeth, using the voice she speaks in when she is talking to parents, not the quiet hissing one she uses to address me.

'Aren't you a dream?' says Mum. 'I'm not sure Mariel has even seen the inside of a library.'

'Mum!' I groan, although it's Elspeth I'm really angry with for getting away with this act.

'This is our flat,' says Uncle Sewell, indicating a green door on the ground floor of a three-storey block. 'Most of these apartments are shared by five students but we get one between the four of us.'

'And you don't have a problem with the noise? I remember what I was like in my student days,' says Mum.

'There is the occasional raucous party, yes, but they're pretty considerate on the whole. Besides, the administrator tends to put third-year students taking mine or Dee's subjects nearby so it's in their best interests to keep on our good side.'

We go inside.

'Mariel, you'll be sleeping in Elspeth's room. Elspeth is moving in with her sister to make space for you.'

I put my bag inside the room, which is filled with shelves of old-fashioned dolls in long Victorian dresses.

'Keep your hands off my stuff,' whispers Elspeth in my ear.

'Some of the dolls in Elspeth's collection are quite valuable,' says Uncle Sewell. 'Lynda, you'll be sleeping in the study.' He places Mum's bag in a small room lined with books.

'Thank you for putting us up,' she says. 'I can't tell you what it means to me after all this time.'

Uncle Sewell smiles kindly and takes Mum's hand. It doesn't make sense to me that she would cut all her brothers out of our lives when she seems to get on with them all.

Lily and Elspeth go into Lily's room, closing the door behind them. I follow Mum and Uncle Sewell into the living room, which is connected to an open-plan kitchen. There is a huge bookshelf along one wall.

'Cup of tea?' asks Uncle Sewell.

'Sounds lovely,' replies Mum.

With both of them looking the other way, I pull out the book and slip it between two boring-looking academic books on the shelf, memorising which ones, then quickly sit down on a sofa.

I hear the front door and a moment later Aunt Dee appears, wearing a colourful headscarf. She is carrying a load of books under one arm and a laptop under the other.

'Hey, Lynda, Mariel. I'm sorry I couldn't come to meet you but my publisher is hounding me to deliver this blasted book.'

'You're writing a book?' I say.

'Yes, and apparently my readership, which consists of eight other similarly qualified academics, four of whom have contributed, are all clamouring to read it at once.'

'What's it called?' asks Mum.

'A *Sociological Study of the Gender Implications of Family Structures*. A sure-fire bestseller, wouldn't you say?'

'It sounds very interesting,' says Mum politely.

Elspeth comes in holding one of her creepy dolls.

'They all get tired of hearing about it around here, don't you?' says Aunt Dee.

Elspeth does an exaggerated yawn but smiles at her mum to indicate that she's only pretending to be bored and sits down next to me.

'Never,' cries Uncle Sewell as he pours boiling water into a teapot.

'What's it about?' asks Mum.

'Basically each family has a set structure but one which is always changing.' Aunt Dee is obviously pleased to have someone new to tell about it. 'My contention is that each time that structure changes, through birth, death, divorce or marriage, the gender of the addition or subtraction is always a key factor to the success of that family unit.'

'How do you measure the success of a family?' asks Mum.

'I set different categories to evaluate success: financial, social, propagation and so on.'

'And how do you prove something like that?'

'I use a range of case studies to look for patterns and draw conclusions.'

'You should use us lot for one of your case studies,' says Mum.

'Ah, now the Considines are what I call a honeybee family, in which one elderly figure – frequently, but not exclusively, a female – holds a powerful grip over the rest of the family, just like the queen bee in a hive.'

'I'm never convinced by this argument,' interrupts Uncle Sewell.

'Neither you nor any of your brothers have ever lived more than ten miles from their mother. What's not convincing?'

'That's not true. Kitson lived in France, Harkett spent all that time in Dubai and we met in the States.'

'And yet, after your father's death you've all ended up back in Wilderdale.'

Uncle Sewell starts to say something about property prices but Aunt Dee interrupts. 'Remember when we were going to take those jobs at the university in London and your mother became desperately ill. She got miraculously better after we decided to stay, didn't she?'

'And what am I in your honeybee structure, Dee?' asks Mum.

'You've adopted the role of rebel, what I term an elected subtraction. In other words you're the bee who escaped the hive. And is it a coincidence you're the only female born into the family? I don't think so.'

'I never wanted to leave. It was her,' replies Mum.

Elspeth leans forward and whispers in my ear so no one else can hear, 'The weak kept alive and the hive can survive, but if they're thrown out of the hive, the hive will thrive.' She sits back sweetly and straightens her doll's dress.

'As another female your mother saw you as a threat,' Aunt Dee is saying enthusiastically.

Uncle Sewell carries the tea tray over and says, 'You did always get on better with Dad than Mum.'

'Didn't we all?' asks Mum.

'You left straight after his funeral. None of us ever knew why,' says Uncle Sewell, handing her a cup of tea. 'Mum just carried on like you never existed but the rest of us were left wondering what we'd done.'

'It wasn't because of you.'

'Then why did you do it?' asks Uncle Sewell. 'What made you run away from not just her, but the rest of your family?'

Mum goes quiet for a moment. She looks at me then back at him. 'It was because of Dad not Mum,' she says.

'You argued with Dad?' says Uncle Sewell.

'No. Dad told me to leave.'

'When?'

'The day before he died.'

Uncle Sewell and Aunt Dee look stunned by this. Elspeth appears more interested in brushing her doll's hair than in the conversation around her.

'What did he say?' I demand. 'Move to Australia, change your name and never speak to your family again?'

'Something like that, yes,' replies Mum.

'Why would he do that?' asks Uncle Sewell.

Mum looks down. 'He was terrified of her. I mean, we were all scared of her when she got angry but towards the end he was really terrified. You were all living elsewhere so you didn't see it but I was staying at home at the time. The day before he died, he took me aside and said that if he was to suddenly die I was to take Mariel far away, and sever all contact with the family. For her safety, he said, to protect her.'

'Protect me from what?' I ask.

'He didn't say but I knew he meant from her, from Mum.'

'And that's why we left?' I say.

Mum nods silently, tears in her eyes. No one knows what to say.

'I've got a question about honeybee families, Mum,' says Elspeth, apparently unaware of Mum's revelation. 'What happens when the queen bee dies?'

'Well,' says Aunt Dee. 'Sometimes the bond between others remains strong, sometimes it weakens and the family fragments. But most often another family member, frequently another female replaces the central figure as the head of the family.'

'That's really interesting, Mummy,' says Elspeth, getting up and taking her doll back to her room.

11

ACUTE MISANTHROPY

For lunch, Uncle Sewell makes us sandwiches on homemade bread. Unlike Aunt Ruth and Aunt Celeste, he doesn't seem as thrown by my not eating meat.

'Dee and I sometimes toy with the idea of giving up meat,' he says. 'It's so much more environmentally friendly. The girls won't hear of it though. They're carnivores through and through.'

As I eat my sandwich, Elspeth pulls out a piece of ham and dangles it in front of my face. 'Meat makes us strong,' she whispers in my ear.

'Meat is murder,' I reply.

She giggles.

After lunch the others settle in the living room. I can't get the book without being seen so I decide to go for a walk.

It's a bright day and the snow that covers the college grounds has melted a little, making it slushy and slippery underfoot. There aren't many people around, although a few lights are on in the flats and I can hear televisions and music from students' bedrooms.

I think about what Mum said. Why would Grandad have sent her away like that? Why would Grandma want to harm me? It doesn't make sense.

'Having a nice walk?' says a voice behind me.

I turn around to see Elspeth.

'Leave me alone, you little freakoid,' I say.

'Grandad was right to send you and your mummy away, you know. Grandma hated you both.'

'You don't know that,' I reply.

'I was Grandma's favourite. She told me things she didn't tell the others.'

'Have you really followed me just to tell me that?'

'No, I'm going up to the roof. Wanna come?'

Metal stairs run up the outside of the building. Elspeth slips under the sign saying, *Fire Escape: Use in Emergencies Only.*

'No thanks.'

'Don't be scared. The students go up there all the time. They're not supposed to but they still do. You can see for miles up there.'

'I'm not scared. You're just the last person I want to spend time with.'

I wonder what it is with my cousins trying to make me climb high things.

'Suit yourself.'

Elspeth runs up the steps. I turn and spot Mum walking towards me. I'm in no mood to talk to her and begin to walk away but she runs after me, calling my name.

'Mariel, please.'

I stop and let her catch up.

'Is everything you've ever told me a lie?' I ask before she can say anything.

'I never told you much. I thought the less I said the fewer lies I'd have to tell.'

'This is your explanation? This is the best you can do?'

'I only wanted to protect you.'

'What, from my grandma? Do you know how mental that sounds?'

'I wanted to protect you from the fear I've had to live with every single day of my life.'

'Grandma loved all my cousins so much she left them her house. Why was I any different? Why did I need protecting from her?'

Mum starts to cry. 'I don't know. He died before he could give me an explanation.'

'How convenient,' I say before I can stop myself.

'There was nothing convenient about his death,' says Mum, sobbing.

My frustration has bubbled up into white rage. 'So we went into hiding because of a silly old man?'

'Your grandfather was a kind, gentle and honest

man. He wouldn't have told me to leave without good reason. Your grandmother felt very differently towards my brothers and their children but from the day I was born she always hated me.'

'I'm beginning to know how she felt,' I reply.

The words hang in the air. I am furious with her. I hate how she has lied to me and how she has kept me away from my grandma. But the feelings die away when I see the hurt look on her face.

'I love you, Mare,' she says. 'We don't need to feel scared any more. We can start again. We've got our family back. I didn't know how it would be, coming back, but everyone has been so nice and welcoming, and we're safe now.'

'I don't feel safe. My cousins are all barking mad.'

'What on earth are you talking about?'

'Oberon tried to make me climb Percy's Ruin, Gerald and Lily keep telling me to stay away, Amelia has that funny smell, and Elspeth is the devil in pigtails.'

'Now come on, Mariel, I know meeting all these new family members must be difficult but that's not fair, and it's very cruel of you to talk about Amelia like that. I thought you two got on.'

'We did, but I've never heard of that condition she's supposed to have.'

'I didn't realise you were an expert on genetics,' Mum says sarcastically. 'Perhaps while there's a library so near you should actually use it. And as for Elspeth, she's probably just having difficulty adjusting to having a new cousin. She's much younger than you.'

'That's another thing. It's weird how close they are. They don't have any friends, you know? None of them. Just each other.'

'So that's what this is all about, is it? You're jealous that they've grown up with all this family and you've been stuck with no one but me.'

This infuriates me because as usual she's making it about herself and has completely misunderstood my point so I say, 'Yes, it is because I only had you and you turned out to be a liar.'

My heart is still pounding from the argument with Mum when Uncle Sewell opens the front door to me. 'Your mum went out to find you,' he says.

'She found me,' I snap.

I follow him inside.

'You shouldn't be too angry with her,' he says. 'She only did what she thought best. Being a good parent and doing the right thing aren't always the same.' We go into the living room. 'The tortured author is in the study,' he says with a wink.

'I heard that,' shouts Aunt Dee.

He returns to the kitchen and continues preparing dinner.

'Why would Grandad have told Mum to run away all those years ago?' I ask.

'I don't know. We all assumed that it was something between your mum and Flora. Our parents were pretty strict and your grandmother never saw eye to eye with your mother, but I don't know why Dad would think she might want to hurt either of you.'

'Did Grandma ever mention me to you?' I ask.

Uncle Sewell picks up a knife and a clove of garlic. 'I'm sorry, Mariel. I suppose trying to forget you was her way of coping with losing you.' He peels the garlic and carefully slices it. 'We're all glad you're both back now though.'

'We'll be flying home in a few days' time,' I say.

'Yes, but we can stay in contact now. And Australia's not so far away. We'll come and visit you. Aren't you pleased to have your family back again?'

'I'm still getting used to it to be honest,' I reply.

He picks up an onion. 'I thought we'd all join you in a meatless meal tonight with a vegetable risotto. The girls will complain, of course, but they can't always have it all their own way, can they?'

With his back turned I extract the book from the bookshelf and sit down with it. Uncle Sewell puts the radio on. It's a classical music station. I consider taking the diary to Elspeth's room but decide there is more danger she will walk in on me. Here, at least, if I hear the front door there is time to hide it. I slip it inside a magazine from the coffee table.

I turn to the first page. The handwriting that fills the pages is a hurriedly written scrawl.

I don't know why I am writing this. I don't know exactly what it is. Is it a diary? Not quite. A diary would contain an account of my daily activities and this will not. Is it a confession? No. A confession requires an audience and I can never show this to anyone. And besides, what would I be confessing to? The things I have seen, the killings I have executed, the murders I have witnessed? No, that is not why I am writing. If anything, I am seeking to understand the curse itself from which I suffer, not the actions it causes. A medical journal, perhaps then, documenting this terrible condition that infects my blood.

'Hello Mariel.' Aunt Dee interrupts my reading. She goes into the kitchen and kisses Uncle Sewell on the cheek. I quickly close the journal and slip it under the sofa seat-cushion.

'How's it going?' asks Uncle Sewell.

'You were right, I'm a tortured author. We should alert Amnesty International,' she says. 'Smells good in here.'

She joins me on the sofa. 'How are you feeling?' she asks.

'I don't know,' I answer honestly.

'Well, you should be grateful your mother kept you away from your grandmother,' she says gently. 'I wish I had been.'

'Why? What was wrong with her?'

'I don't know if it has a medical name.' She laughs. 'Acute misanthropy?'

'What does that mean?'

'A misanthropist is someone who hates people. Flora hated everyone, except her precious grand-children, of course.' Hearing the front door, Aunt Dee says quickly, 'You can't say a bad word about her in front of them. They'll bite your head off.'

Mum enters with Elspeth. They exchange a glance and Elspeth walks over and addresses me in a clear, loud voice.

'Mariel, I owe you an apology. I haven't been as friendly as I could have been. There is no excuse for my behaviour but there are reasons for it. When we first met, I was upset about Grandma dying. Then I became worried because I'm the youngest of my cousins and I often feel left out and I thought that with another older cousin I'd feel even more left out. So I'm very sorry I haven't been nice to you. Can you forgive me?'

She flings herself on the sofa and throws her arms around me.

'Mariel, what do you say?' I could kill Mum for saying this and for talking to Elspeth in the first place.

'That's OK, Elspeth, I forgive you.' It chokes me to say it but what choice do I have? I've been manipulated by an eight-year-old. Elspeth squeezes me so hard it hurts.

12

A ROOFTOP ENCOUNTER

More snow falls in the afternoon so everyone stays in the living room, preventing me from retrieving the diary from its new hiding place. That evening when we sit down to dinner Elspeth grumbles about the lack of meat but Lily says nothing. The risotto is nice though and I am grateful to Uncle Sewell for making it. At the end of the meal I take the dishes into the kitchen to load them into the dishwasher. Elspeth helps me, but once we are out of earshot she whispers, 'Did you like my speech, half-cousin?'

'It was very convincing,' I reply.

She laughs and goes back to the table.

For the rest of the evening, Aunt Dee dominates the conversation. She appears to have an opinion on everything and she, Mum and Uncle Sewell argue about politics and other boring stuff. I am itching to rescue the diary from the sofa but I can't risk it until I am sure no one is looking. I decide the safest thing to do is to wait until they have all gone to bed.

One of Aunt Dee's many opinions is that children should be allowed to choose their own bedtime so I am the first to use the bathroom and go to bed.

'Touch any of my stuff and you're dead,' threatens Elspeth before adding loudly, 'Sleep well, Mariel. See you in the morning.'

I close the door and wait until everyone has gone to bed. Mum doesn't come to say goodnight. I have never felt so distant from her. Since we landed in England it feels like she and I have been living two different stories. The adults chat casually amongst themselves, while their children whisper at me. I have spent all my life dreaming of what it would be like to have a large family, but now I have one I feel more alone than I have ever felt.

Elspeth's dolls stare down at me. Some wear bonnets, others too much make-up. Many of them have patchy skin, worn away by time. They all look deeply sinister and I can see no reason to collect them other than to freak people out.

I hear a rustling from the door and notice that a piece of paper has been slipped under it. I pick it up and read it.

If you want to know what is wrong with us, wait for three taps on the window, then leave quietly through the window and go to where Elspeth tried to take you today. I will explain everything.

Lily

PS Do not leave your room or open your curtains before then.

I read the note twice. *What is wrong with us,* it says. Not what is wrong with Elspeth. What is wrong with us. I think about the words in the diary. *This terrible condition that infects my blood.* The house is quiet. It is the perfect moment to go and get the diary but Lily's note said not to leave my room and I so desperately want to know the truth.

Elspeth's dolls are creeping me out. I think that if I slept every night in this room I would be as disturbed as she is. I need something to distract me from them so I get up to look for a book to read. I check the drawers and find one full of silver jewellery, just like at Grandma's house and in Amelia's room. One of the bits looks familiar. It's a silver crucifix. I reach into my bag and pull out the identical one I found on the hill. What does it mean, I wonder?

The three taps on the window are quiet but they still make me jump. I draw the curtains and look out but all I see is my own reflection. I turn off the light. No one's there. I push open the window and feel the cold. The external lighting gives the university campus an eerie yellow glow. I put on my coat, climb up on to the window ledge and jump out.

The moon is big and low in the sky. The snow crunches beneath my feet as I walk to the fire escape that leads to the roof. I swing under the chain and go up.

The steps have iced over so I have to grip the cold railing. On each floor a door with a glass panel reveals a long deserted corridor behind it. I can hear music playing and students talking.

At the top of the building is a flat roof with a waist-high wall around the edge from which I can see how close the university is to Chilton. In the other direction I can make out the thin outline of Percy's Ruin at the top of the hill. There is no fire on top tonight.

'Lily?' I whisper in case she's hiding in the shadows.

There is no reply. I turn around, thinking she must be behind me.

It is not immediately obvious what I am looking at but it isn't Lily's silhouette. Its edges are jagged and it is too large. It turns slightly and I see a head with a long dog-like nose. It opens its mouth and I catch sight of glistening white teeth. The creature steps down from the wall and moves towards me. It walks on all fours. Its body is covered in hair. It looks up and light spills on to its face. Its mouth curls at the corners. I recognise that smile and even though the whites of its eyes are bright red, I recognise those brown eyes and that twitching nose. In spite of his current form I am in no doubt as to who it is.

'Oberon,' I gasp.

I wonder if it could be some silly joke, but this is not a fancy-dress costume. His face is still recognisable but his chin is extended and his nose is now black. Patchy hair has sprung up around his face and below his wolfish ears. A fat pink tongue licks the outside of his teeth. 'Hi, cuz,' he growls.

He steps forward.

I step back.

'You scared?'

'No,' I lie.

'Surprised then?'

I gather myself. 'Not really. From your table manners I knew you were an animal. I just figured it was a pig rather than a . . .' I still can't bring myself to say it.

'A wolf.' He finishes my sentence triumphantly.

'What do you want with me?'

'Want?' he says, with a low breathy laugh. 'I want to chew on your weak vegetarian heart and wash it down with your watery human blood. But that would be messy and we're in a public place so I'll have to settle for breaking your neck and making it look like you fell to your death. You were smart not to go up Percy's Ruin but now you're here and there's nowhere to run.'

He backs me into a corner. 'Why would you want to kill me?'

'Oh, come on, it will be a painless way to die. Much better than being torn apart, don't you think?'

He pushes his face up close to mine and, with all my strength, I punch him on the side of his nose. He growls and swipes my hand. It takes a moment for the pain to register but I look down and see he has drawn blood.

'You ready to die now?'

'She's my prey.'

Oberon swings his head round to see who has spoken but I have already identified it as Elspeth's whisper. She steps on to the roof and I see that she too has undergone a transformation. Her facial features have been stretched into a new shape. Her body is covered in hair. She too is a wolf.

She says, 'You had your chance at the tower. A pathetic, cowardly attempt to kill the half-cousin. Not even at night, not even in our true form. Lazy wolf.'

Oberon growls. 'She's not yours.'

'My note brought her up here so she's mine.'

'I'm pack leader. You should obey me.'

'When the moon is full and our victims bleed, then we'll decide who will lead.'

Oberon lurches forward, his jaws snapping and a low growl sounding from the back of his throat. Elspeth dodges his attack but he comes at her again, jumping up and landing heavily, narrowly missing her. Oberon is larger and stronger but there is something deadly about Elspeth's fluid movements and, while she is moving out of his way, she reaches out a claw and scratches his large belly.

'Mariel, come this way,' a girl's voice whispers to me from the stairs.

I move towards it though I cannot see who it is. Oberon and Elspeth are too preoccupied to notice.

'You should accept me as pack leader now Ma'wolf is gone,' says Oberon.

'Ma'wolf would never have wanted you to be our leader, you clumsy oaf,' hisses Elspeth.

'Kills are all that matters and I have more than any of you.'

'Killing cows then falling asleep in the barn. Hardly the act of a leader. Greedy fat wolf.' Elspeth spits out the words.

The two fight again and this time Oberon manages to pin Elspeth down for a couple of seconds before she wriggles free.

I climb over the wall to the top of the stairs.

'Follow me down.' It's Lily's voice.

I head down as fast as I can but Oberon and Elspeth have noticed. They land on the stairs above me. In my hurry I lose my footing on the icy steps and fall awkwardly. My spine screams out in pain but I have no time to listen to it. I run, fall, stumble and slide down. They are close. I can barely think for fear.

I reach the bottom but in front of me is another wolfish face. It is Lily. The hair that covers her body is jet black. She grabs me and throws me on to her back, bringing me face to face with Oberon and Elspeth, who are standing in the stairwell snarling.

'You will not harm her tonight,' says Lily.

Elspeth and Oberon growl, but they say nothing.

'Hold tight.' Lily turns and runs.

Holding on is tricky because, although she is clearly strong enough to carry me, she is smaller than me and my feet drag on the icy ground as she runs. When we reach the flat, I climb off and look at her. She has no fringe to hide behind in this form. She looks away and says, 'Give me a minute to change before you follow me in.' She says it casually, like she's changing her dress, rather than transforming from a wolf into a human. 'Don't worry, they wouldn't risk making trouble this close to the flat.' She climbs through the window, moving easily and naturally on all fours.

Standing outside on my own I feel a tide of emotions wash over me. I can't take it all in. It doesn't make sense.

'You can come in now,' says Lily.

Inside the room, she keeps the lights off but I can see that she is back to her human self with her black hair covering half her face. She has put on a dressing gown.

'We don't have long,' she says, drawing the curtains.

'Will she come back?'

'Soon but not straight away. They're both so worked up they won't be able to sleep until they've killed.'

'Killed what?'

'Probably a forest creature, a rabbit or a vole. That's what we normally do. That's what Ma'wolf taught us to do.'

'Ma'wolf?'

'Grandma was pack leader. She taught us that pets and farm animals attract too much attention. Forest creatures go unnoticed.'

'What about Farmer Dooley's cow?' I say.

Lily nods. 'That was stupid of Oberon.'

'And the Alsatian that Kitson treated?'

'Freddie's fault. He said it was self-defence but he should have known better.'

'And are you all . . .' I pause. It feels ridiculous to say the words out loud but what else can I say? 'Are you all werewolves?'

Lily nods. 'You're bleeding,' she says, noticing my hand.

I had forgotten about the cut. 'A scratch,' I say. 'Isn't that how you become a werewolf?'

'Please don't use that word. We are wolves. And no, it doesn't work like that. Here, wrap this around it.'

She passes me a piece of cloth from a drawer and I bind my wound.

'How does it happen then?'

'It's called the Lycan gene. It's passed down through families.'

'But I'm family.'

'You're different. You don't have it.'

'What about our parents?'

'No. None of them.'

'And they don't know?'

'Ma'wolf was always careful to keep it a secret.'

'They must suspect something?'

She looks at me wearily. 'Did you before you saw it with your own eyes?'

'No, well, I mean, I thought about the idea but . . . no. I still don't understand. It's not even a full moon tonight.'

'The moon has power over us but it only needs to be night for us to change.'

'So why do you change?'

'Once the wolf is inside, you can't ignore the voice. It has needs.'

'What do they want with me?'

Lily sighs. 'When Ma'wolf died, we were left without a pack leader.'

'Oberon said he was leader.'

'He said that because he's got the most kills, but it isn't as simple as that. There are other factors.'

'Like what?'

'Like the quality of the kill. The larger, stronger the animal, the higher the value.'

'And the highest is human?' I say.

'The highest is a member of your own family,' she

replies. 'Which makes you an easy target. You have the same grandparents as us but you are not one of us.'

I think about what Mum said about her reasons for leaving. Grandad must have known about Grandma. He wanted to save me. That must have been why he sent us away.

'So they'll keep trying to kill me?'

'If you stay indoors, you'll be safe. None of them will risk being found out, despite what my sister says. In a few days you'll be gone and you'll be safe.'

'And no one knows about this?'

'No. It's been kept secret for generations. You can't tell anyone. If you did, you wouldn't just have Elspeth to fear. If I thought you were going to let the secret out, I would kill you myself.' Lily pushes back her hair and meets my gaze with both eyes. Even though she is human now and the whites of her eyes are no longer red, I can see the wolf in her. 'Keeping it secret is the only thing that allows us to live normal lives by day.'

Outside, in the distance, one of them howls.

'She's made her kill,' says Lily. 'You have to go to bed now before she returns.'

'Why aren't you like them?'

'I am.'

'But you saved me.'

'Don't make me regret it.'

13

YOUNG LOVE AND OLD FRIENDS

I lie wide awake for the rest of the night, watching the door, listening out for Elspeth's return and trying to understand everything that has happened. My cousins are werewolves. My grandma was the pack leader, deceiving her own children and teaching her grand-children how to hunt and kill. What kind of woman would do that? Grandmas are supposed to be kind. They are supposed to like knitting and cups of tea. They aren't supposed to turn their grandchildren into vicious killing animals.

I wonder what other confessions her diary contains. I try to force myself out of the room but fear binds me to the bed. The night passes slowly. I try to imagine how my other cousins look as wolves. Amelia is the hardest to picture; she is so pretty and stylish, it is difficult to imagine her covered in hair with a long dog-like nose and sharp white teeth.

Only as daylight is creeping around the side of the blind do I finally fall asleep. When I wake up, the clock on Elspeth's wall says it's midday. I get out of bed and go into the living room.

Aunt Dee is sitting on the sofa, a laptop on her knee, surrounded by pieces of paper and open books. She is sitting on the cushion that hides Grandma's diary.

'Afternoon. You slept well.' She laughs.

It has been the worst night of my life but I nod and ask where everyone else is.

'Sewell and your mum have gone to the farmers' market. The girls were driving me mad with their bickering so I sent them too. Honestly, you would think they'd be able to share for two nights without being at each other's throats.' The words conjure up a different image to the one she intends. 'You don't mind getting your own breakfast, do you? I think I'm on the final furlong and there's light at the end of the tunnel. That's a mixed metaphor but you know what I mean.'

I make myself cereal, then take a shower. I wish there was some noise in the house, a TV on or some music playing, anything to distract me from the terrible flashes of memory from last night. Every time I close my eyes I see Oberon's hungry wolf face in front of me. In the shower I peel off the bandage on my hand. It still feels tender but the wound is barely visible now. I am brushing my teeth when the doorbell rings.

'Mariel, would you mind getting that?' shouts Aunt Dee. 'If it's anyone for me, I'm not in.'

I quickly pull on my jeans and T-shirt and go to the door. Father Gowlett is standing on the doorstep. He adjusts his glasses and says. 'Oh, hello again. I was actually hoping to have a word with Dee.'

'She's not in,' I lie.

He smiles and says in a loud voice, 'Or she's in there working on her book but doesn't want to be disturbed.'

From the living room, Aunt Dee shouts, 'You know me too well, Ben.'

Father Gowlett winks at me. 'Oh well, could you pass on a message for me? Could you say that I am happy to babysit for Lily and Elspeth on Wednesday night?'

'OK.'

His eyes light up and he adds loudly, 'Actually tell her I'll babysit on condition she comes to church tomorrow?'

'Not a chance,' shouts Aunt Dee. 'Tell him to stop God-bothering you.'

He laughs and says to me, 'She's not a big fan of religion, your aunt, but I always say that the godless need us more than believers do.'

'What about Grandma? Did she believe?' I ask.

'Flora believed in family.'

'You knew my grandma well, didn't you?'

'Oh yes, Flora moved to Wilderdale when I was a young man.'

'What was she like?'

Father Gowlett considers this and says, 'Intriguing. She was an intriguing woman.'

There is something in the way he says it that makes me think he knows more than he is letting on.

'I'll let you into a secret,' he says. He bends down to speak in my ear and, for a moment, I wonder what he is going to say. 'When we were young, your grandmother and I courted.' He chuckles. 'That's what it was called back then. Dating, I suppose you'd say these days. I actually proposed to her once.'

'What did she say?'

He straightens up. 'She said she couldn't marry me because she had fallen in love with my best friend. That was your grandfather.'

'You were best friends?'

'All our lives. Even after he stole Flora from me.'

'What was Grandad like?'

'Frank was cleverer, fitter, stronger and richer than me. He even married the girl I loved, and yet he was impossible to hate. A true gent was Frank. I lost a great friend when he died. It was a terrible way to go.'

'Why? How did he die?'

'Your mother never told you?'

'She told me he died, she never told me how.'

'Oh well, I shouldn't be the one then.'

'I want to know.'

Father Gowlett shuffles his feet and then answers. 'A burglar broke into Louvre House. Frank went downstairs to confront him. In the struggle he was killed. Luckily for you the burglar fled.'

'Why was that lucky for me?' I ask.

'You and your mother were staying with your grand-parents at the time. Your mother, the poor dear, was the one who found his body on the kitchen floor.'

'Where was Grandma?'

'She slept through the whole thing.'

I imagine the scene: Mum coming downstairs to find her father dead, crying or screaming before running upstairs to check on me, still sleeping in my cot. Her own mother waking up to find her husband had been killed. The image appears vividly in my mind almost like I can actually remember it. It is another thing Mum has kept from me, but I can't blame her for this one.

'I must go now, but why don't you come to my service tomorrow?' says Father Gowlett.

I agree to go because it feels to me like there are other questions I need to ask him. Once he has gone, I finish getting dressed, then head outside. I'm not really going anywhere in particular but I find myself at the library. It has large windows and sliding doors. There is an information desk with a bored-looking student sitting behind it, reading a book. I ask him for the section on Genetics.

'Science books are on the second floor,' he replies, barely looking up from his book.

There are a few students dotted around the library, mostly sitting at computers. The Genetics section, however, is empty. I pull out several dull-looking books. There is nothing in the index about a Lycan gene. Under 'W' there is reference to a werewolf gene but when I turn to the page it is a condition called 'hypertrichosis', which causes extreme hair growth in people. There is a picture of a man whose entire body, including his face is covered in hair, which is pretty weird but a long way from what I witnessed last night. The man in the picture looks sad so I don't linger on it. I try reading up on how genes work but it is full of long technical words which I can't understand. I return the book to the shelf, and go and find a computer. An internet search brings up more pictures of the sad-looking man and others with his condition. There are also websites of werewolf fanatics who call themselves Lycans and lots of pages saying the usual stuff about full moons and silver bullets, but I find nothing about an actual genetic condition so I log off and leave the library.

Back at the flat, the door has been left on the latch and I can hear laughter from inside. As I enter, Uncle Sewell, Aunt Dee, Lily, Elspeth and Mum all cheer and raise their glasses. Aunt Dee crosses the room to hand me a glass. 'Ah, Mariel. We're celebrating. I've written the last sentence.'

Uncle Sewell pours me a glass of grape juice.

'Now we're all here, may I propose a toast,' he says. 'Ladies and gentlemen, boys and girls, raise your glasses please to my extremely clever wife, Professor Dee Considine.'

'Speech . . . speech,' shout Lily and Elspeth, giggling.

'No no no, oh, all right then,' says Aunt Dee. 'Thank you everyone for your love and support and for helping me write another unreadable book to be unread by a select number of uninteresting intellectuals.'

We all clink glasses and Mum puts her arm round me. Without meaning to, I flinch at her touch. There is so much she hasn't told me and yet there is so much she doesn't know. I look into her eyes and it feels like I'm looking at a stranger . . .

'Isn't this nice?' she says.

Elspeth and Lily are laughing and acting like normal sisters in a normal family. How can they live two such different lives? How can they be one thing at night and something so different by day? The secret burns inside of me. I feel it tightening around my chest, crushing me from within, separating me from everything else. I glance over at the sofa but there is no chance of me retrieving the diary without being seen. Lily meets my gaze and looks at me.

'It's been a lovely couple of days,' says Mum. 'It's a shame Mariel wasn't awake in time to come to the farmers' market this morning.'

'Mariel had to stay here and protect me from the God squad,' says Aunt Dee.

'Gowlett?' says Uncle Sewell.

'Yes, he says he can babysit on Wednesday.'

'We don't need a babysitter. We're old enough to look after ourselves,' says Elspeth.

'Not a chance,' replies Aunt Dee.

'I'd like to go to church tomorrow,' I say.

'You've never been to church in your life,' says Mum.

'I haven't lived all my life yet,' I reply.

For dinner Uncle Sewell cooks a large joint of beef bought from the market. He cooks it medium rare so that it is pink and fleshy in the middle. When he offers a slice to Mum, she says it's too rare for her and asks for a cut from the side instead.

'I'll have the middle bit,' says Elspeth, catching my eye. 'I like my meat bloody.'

No one else notices the dark tone in her voice.

I feel pleased this is the last night with her. I need to retrieve the book before we leave in the morning so after everyone has gone to bed I get up and sneak out. I push open the living room door and stop dead because a light is on. Lily is sitting on the sofa. She has the diary in her hands. She looks up at me and mouths for me to close the door.

'Where did you find it?' she whispers.

'Behind the painting,' I reply.

'How much have you read?'

'Just the first page. It's Grandma's diary, isn't it?'

Lily closes the book. 'Yes.'

'I'd like to read more,' I say.

'No.'

'But I found it.'

'You shouldn't have been looking. You shouldn't know anything about us. If people knew about us, it would endanger the whole species.'

'There are others?' I ask.

It hasn't occurred to me that there might be other families who carry the gene.

'Of course there are others, but you need to forget everything you know.'

I sit down next to her. 'Grandad must have known about her. That must have been why he sent Mum away.'

'It doesn't matter. It's the past.'

I think about the picture of my grandparents on their wedding day. 'Do you think he knew when he married her?'

'I don't know. Grandma never talked about him.' Lily's tone is clipped like she wants me to stop asking these questions.

'If you let me look at the diary, I promise to give it back and not to tell.' I reach out my hand but Lily leaves it hanging there.

'Tomorrow I'm going to burn this diary. I can't let it fall into the wrong hands.'

'Like whose?'

'There are people out there who want evidence of our existence. They set up traps and cameras in the woods.'

'What people?'

She looks away. 'You should go to bed. Elspeth will be back soon.'

'She's gone out to kill again?'

Lily's silence answers my question.

'And you? Will you kill tonight?' I ask.

She looks down. 'We all kill. We can't not. You can't ignore the voice.'

'Don't you feel bad about it?' I ask.

'It's nature. Big animals kill little ones,' she replies.

'And you eat what you kill or you just hunt for fun?'

'It's not fun,' says Lily. 'Not for me anyway. But you've seen what we're like after the change. We don't just change on the outside. Killing becomes instinct. Our stomachs crave fresh raw meat. And it will be your meat if Elspeth finds out you know about the diary.'

14

THE SUNDAY SERVICE

When Mum and I say goodbye, Lily and Elspeth are polite but quiet. No one would suspect from their behaviour that during my two-day stay one of them threatened to kill me and the other actually tried to do so.

Uncle Sewell drives us off the campus to drop me at the church before taking Mum to pick up the hire car. Both of them are keen to avoid the embarrassment of having to explain to Father Gowlett why they are not attending his sermon so they drop me off around the corner from the church.

Another day of sunshine has reduced the snow covering in the churchyard to a few grubby-looking clumps but it is still cold and icicles hang from the church roof.

I am the youngest member of the congregation by a long way and Father Gowlett does a good job of hiding his disappointment at the small turnout. He reads some prayers and delivers a sermon about being kind to one another. The hymns we sing are tuneless dirges, accompanied by the old lady on the organ and her yapping dog, who I recognise from Grandma's funeral. When Father Gowlett finally says my Grandma's name, it is as part of a long list of other local people who have recently died.

At the end, he stands by the door and shakes everyone's hands. I stay longer on the bench and follow the old organist up the aisle.

'Now, Mrs Mills,' he says to the old woman. 'I really would prefer if you were to leave Mr Pickles at home. I know he likes to join in with the hymns, but I feel he may not have picked up on some of the subtler points of my sermon.'

'I'm sorry, Father. I thought I had left him but the naughty thing climbs into my bag when I'm not looking. I think he likes it here. He finds your voice very soothing.'

'That's nice to hear but, as I say, perhaps next time you could check inside your bag before leaving the house.'

The old lady moves on and Father Gowlett peers down at me, his pale eyes magnified by his glasses. 'Mariel. Thank you for coming.'

'I have more questions about my grandparents.'

'Of course. Do you mind if I tidy up as we talk?'

I follow him back into the church. He gathers up the rows of hymn books he has laid out.

'You said a burglar killed Grandad all those years ago,' I say.

'That's right.'

'Exactly how did Grandad die?'

He coughs and says, 'I shouldn't want to be the cause of nightmares.'

'I don't have nightmares. I'd like to know,' I respond.

'Frank's neck was broken,' he replies.

Both my grandparents died of broken necks. Surely I'm not the only one to find this strange. I remember how Father Gowlett said Grandma slept through the attack. Looking up I realise he is watching me. I meet his gaze and for a moment we understand one another.

'You've discovered their secret, haven't you?' he says.

I don't respond but he can clearly see the relief on my face at having someone to talk to about my cousins. He marches to the door, shuts and locks it. The sound of the heavy bolt echoes around the high ceiling. Even though the church is empty he looks around again to check no one can hear. When he speaks, it is in a low whisper.

'How did you find out?'

'Oberon and Elspeth tried to kill me,' I reply.

His eyes light up with excitement. 'You saw them . . . changed, I mean?'

'Yes.'

A grim smile spreads across his face. 'If one of them were to kill you, it would secure the right to lead the pack. You must keep safe. Who are you staying with next?'

'Freddie.'

'Be careful with him. He's intelligent but ambitious enough to be a danger to you.'

'How do you know about them?'

'I have known for many years. Since before they were born. I saw your grandmother as a wolf once. She was a beautiful creature even in that ungodly form.'

'And she knew you knew?'

'Oh yes. Flora liked to tease me. I tried to persuade her to reveal her secret many times but wolves are secretive by nature. They have been hunted for many centuries. They fear discovery but the world needs to know of their existence.'

'So it was you Lily was talking about, when she said about people setting traps in the woods.'

Father Gowlett shakes his head. 'Flora swore she never told them about me. As far as your cousins are concerned I am just an old family friend.'

'I don't understand. You said you asked her to marry you.'

He flicks through the pages of a hymn book absent-mindedly. 'I was . . .' His pause makes me feel that he is ashamed of what he is about to say. 'I was obsessed with her. I didn't want to lose her. When she said no, I followed her into the woods. She allowed me to see her as a wolf in an attempt to stop me loving her.'

'Did Grandad know before they got married?'

'Yes.'

'Then why did he marry her?'

'Frank loved Flora for all her faults.'

Outside, the sun comes out, illuminating the coloured glass and painting Father Gowlett's wrinkled face a strange tinge of red. 'And yet she rewarded his love by breaking his neck.' He places a heavy hand on my shoulder. 'Yes, Mariel, Flora murdered your grandfather.'

I try to take this in, but I feel disconnected, like a character in the stained-glass window looking down on the two of us talking.

'What about Grandma?' I ask. 'Was her death really an accident?'

'No. She may not have been young any more but she was strong. It would take more than a tumble down some stairs to kill the great Ma'wolf.'

'Then who . . .'

'I believe one of your cousins killed her. This is how it is with them. They are without morals, without humanity. The single biggest threat to a wolf is another wolf in their pack. Time and again they fight among themselves in order to gain control of the pack. Hierarchy is everything to them.'

A knock on the big wooden doors makes both of us jump.

'Anyone in there?' It's Freddie's voice.

Father Gowlett looks at me frantically. 'You mustn't let them know I know. And be careful, Mariel. Your cousins are deadly.'

'But why am I not affected?'

'You're different.'

'That's what Lily said. What do you mean?' He turns to get the door but I grab his sleeve. 'You must tell me.'

He pulls himself free from my grip. 'The gene follows a very specific pattern,' he says.

'What pattern?'

Freddie bangs on the door again.

'Coming!' shouts Father Gowlett. He turns to me and whispers, 'The Lycan gene is passed down through carriers of the opposite sex so it only continued through Flora's sons. But it always skips a generation so none of them have it themselves.'

'But if it's passed down through the opposite sex, shouldn't it only affect the girls?'

'No. Your uncles are all carriers. All of their children, regardless of their sex, may develop the condition.

'Now, I must open the door. Promise me you'll stay indoors at night, Mariel.' Father Gowlett walks up the aisle and throws open the door. Light spills into the church. On the other side of the door Freddie stands in perfect silhouette.

'I was about to find a battering ram and break the

door down.' He laughs. 'Hi, Father. Come on, Mariel, Rob's got the engine running.'

'Rob?' I say.

'My dad,' says Freddie. 'He doesn't like it when I call him dad. Says it makes him feel old.'

Uncle Robson is sitting in the driving seat of a red sports car with music blaring out of the radio. Freddie opens the passenger door and pulls the seat forward to let me climb into the back. I look over my shoulder for Father Gowlett but he has disappeared inside the church.

'How do you like the new set of wheels, Mariel?' asks Uncle Robson.

'Very nice,' I reply.

'Nice?' he yells over the music. 'I pick her up in this limited edition Aston Martin DB5 and she calls it nice.' He laughs.

'It's great,' I say.

Freddie pushes the seat back and sits next to his dad. 'Rob just bought this car. There are only fifty exactly like it in the country.'

'And I don't mind telling you, it cost a fair packet,' shouts Uncle Robson.

'Where's Mum?' I yell back.

'She's back at the flat, probably enjoying the fifty-two-inch widescreen or the jacuzzi we just had installed. Oh yes, you've just upgraded by coming to stay with us. Buckle up.'

Uncle Robson puts his foot on the accelerator and I quickly grab the seat belt and put it on. With the revving engine and the blasting radio, I notice passers-by turning to see what is making the noise as we speed down through the little villages into Chilton.

Freddie swivels round to talk to me but it still doesn't occur to either of them to turn down the music. 'What were you doing at church anyway?' he asks with a mischievous smile.

'Father Gowlett said a prayer for Grandma.'

It surprises me how funny Freddie finds this. 'Grandma used to say the only bit of religion she liked were the sacrifices.' He winks at me and I am in no doubt that the others have told him that I know.

'The problem I have with all that religion stuff is the whole business of waiting for your rewards in heaven,' says Uncle Robson. 'To be honest, I'd rather get my rewards a bit sooner. As I see it, I work hard therefore I've earned the right to a few rewards now, like this car, and wait until you see the flat. We've just had the roof terrace done. We're having a big family get-together up there tomorrow.'

The red light turns to amber and Uncle Robson accelerates so quickly that I am pushed back into my seat.

I am glad when the car finally stops in the underground garage because I am beginning to feel travel-sick. Freddie lifts up the seat and I step out. Next to us is the hire car Mum and I arrived in.

We cross the car park to a lift with a sliding metal grate.

'This place used to be a pea factory,' says Uncle Robson, 'but the company went out of business years ago. It was just a shell when I first found it.'

'A pea shell,' says Freddie. It sounds like a well-rehearsed joke.

I force out a fake laugh.

'Yep, I saw the place had potential,' says Uncle Robson, answering a question I didn't ask. 'A wad of cash, a bit of time and a whole lot of hard work later and the old pea factory is now ten luxury flats in the heart of Chilton. The biggest of which belongs to yours truly.'

'It used to have millions of peas, now it's worth millions of pounds,' adds Freddie.

I wonder how many times they have told this story with the same bad jokes. The lift takes us to the top floor. We step out and I follow them into the flat.

They both turn to look at me for a reaction as we enter and, even though I don't want to be, it is difficult not to be impressed by the flat. It has large windows from the floor to the high ceiling that boast a view of Chilton's skyline. I can see the curve of the canal that runs through its centre. The walls of the flat are decorated with expensive-looking artwork and the biggest flatscreen television I have ever seen. Mum is sitting on a large L-shaped sofa.

'Hello, love,' she says. 'How was church?'

It is such a simple question. But what *is* the answer? I learnt that her mother murdered her father. I discovered that I'm not the only one who knows about my cousins transforming into wild creatures every night. I know the reason her mother cared so little for her and the reason her father warned us to stay away. If only he had explained that it would never be safe to return, even after Grandma's death, then we could have carried on as we were, just the two of us, 'our compact little family unit'. I tell her church was OK.

Freddie shows me the room I'll be sleeping in, which has glass doors that lead out on to a small balcony. I follow him out but I stay away from the edge. I have learnt my lesson about my cousins and heights.

'Don't be nervous,' he says. 'I'm not like Oberon.'

There is no chance of being heard by Mum and Uncle Robson but I am still surprised he refers so casually to Oberon's attempt to kill me. The secret of my cousins' curse doesn't seem to weigh him down like it does the others.

He laughs. 'Even if you did fall, it's not exactly far.'

I see that below the balcony is another part of the building easily near enough to jump to without hurting myself.

'My room's up there.' He points to another balcony above. 'There's a way out over the roofs. I'll show you tonight. You can come with me.'

'That's very kind of you but no thanks,' I say.

'You're not scared are you?'

'Just because two nights ago my cousins turned into wolves and tried to kill me? No, why would I be scared?'

'Listen, Mariel, I can see why Oberon and Elspeth might freak you out but you haven't seen what fun it can be. I'm not going to harm you.'

'I don't want to go anywhere. I'll be just fine here, thanks.'

Uncle Robson appears at the doorway. 'Hey, Fred, I was thinking we'd go out tonight for a bite to eat, show our guests a bit of the nightlife of Chilton.'

'Excellent idea, Rob,' says Freddie. 'I was just saying the same thing.'

15

A NIGHT OUT

The restaurant Uncle Robson takes us to is really smart and all the other customers look like they have a lot of money. The food is so expensive that Mum flinches when she sees the menu. Uncle Robson sees this too and says, 'Don't worry, Lynda. Tonight's on me.' Mum politely protests but gives in soon enough. A waiter brings a bottle of wine and says, 'Would you or your wife like to taste it?' he asks.

Everyone laughs at this and Uncle Robson says that his sister will try the wine, which makes the waiter apologise. Once he has gone Uncle Robson says, 'He must be new. I come here with enough different women.'

'Any potential marriage material?' asks Mum.

'No way. After Sophie and I divorced, I decided that was it for marriage and me.'

Mum says, 'How long ago did you and she split?'

'Freddie was four so however long that is.'

'How did you decide who Freddie stayed with?' she asks.

Uncle Robson takes a sip of wine and says, 'Sophie wanted custody but as you can imagine Mum was pretty fierce about the whole thing.' He puts on a voice and says, 'No grandchild of mine is going to be brought up by a stranger.'

'Did you go to court?' asks Mum.

'No. In the end Sophie agreed to let Freddie decide for himself. It was Mum's idea and she could hardly argue with it. He decided to stay with me. Good job, eh? What did you say her husband drives, Fred?'

'A ten-year-old Ford Focus.'

They both laugh.

Grandma worked so hard to make sure all of her grandchildren stayed nearby and had the ability to slip out of their homes at night.

'You made a four-year-old choose between his parents? That's terrible, Rob,' Mum sounds appalled.

I completely agree with her so I'm surprised to hear myself say, 'It's more choice than I ever had.'

It's an awkward moment and everyone looks grateful when the waiter comes back with our drinks. By the time we've ordered food, the conversation has moved on. During the meal, Uncle Robson and Mum talk while Freddie amuses me by pointing out people in the restaurant and guessing what they are saying, putting on funny voices, some of which make me laugh so much that I snort drink out of my nose, making us both giggle even more. It feels good to laugh. Freddie puts such energy into enjoying himself that it makes it difficult to think about everything else and there are moments when I forget about the horror of Friday night.

After the meal, back at the apartment, Mum stays up with Uncle Robson but I'm tired and go to bed. I want to avoid Freddie until morning but he comes to my room to say goodnight and whispers, 'I'll knock on the window when they've gone to sleep and we'll slip out.'

'No, I told you, I'm not going,' I reply.

'I'll see you later,' he says with a grin. I can tell he thinks he'll be able to persuade me.

I struggle to draw the curtains until I realise there's a button that operates them automatically. I sit on the bed and watch them slowly close, shutting out the moon, which is so big and has such a luminous glow that if I didn't know otherwise I would have said it was full. I press the button and the curtains open, allowing me to look at it again. The face I've seen in it before looks different tonight. It feels like it is staring straight at me. I shut the curtains again and get into bed.

I lie awake for an hour or so, unable to sleep for the anticipation of the tap on the window I know is coming. When it comes, I say, 'Leave me alone,' but Freddie taps again.

I get up, dress and press the button to open the curtain. He is sitting on the ledge. It's Freddie all right but he is no longer human. His body is covered in long brown hair. The whites of his eyes are now red. He smiles. It's strange how even after the change my cousins are recognisably themselves.

'Open the door,' says Freddie.

'Go away,' I say. 'I'm not going anywhere with you.'

'I'm hardly going to attack you here, in my home,' he says.

He's such an amazing-looking creature that I understand why Father Gowlett described my grandma as beautiful. Part of me wants to reach out and touch him, to check that he is real. I slide the door open. The icy night air makes me shiver.

Freddie grins, displaying his long white teeth. 'On Friday afternoon you had no idea this was possible,' he says. 'You lived in the same boring world as everyone else. But Friday night your world got bigger, didn't it? I've known about this since I was five years old, but you . . . You must be questioning everything you thought you knew. And you're telling me you're happy to turn your back on it all and go back to sleep like all these other humans?' He turns his head and motions to the rest of the city.

'How long have you been working on that speech then?' I ask.

Again, the grin. 'About an hour. How was it?'

'Great. I'm not going.'

Freddie stretches his legs and arches his back. In the moonlight I can see not just the hair that covers his body but the curves of his muscles, his strong legs and powerful shoulders.

'Why not?' he says.

'I don't trust you. If you kill me, you can become the pack leader.'

Freddie steps down and brings his face closer to mine. Even as a wolf, there is an attractive symmetry to his features.

'If I had wanted to kill you, I'd have done it when you were sitting in that tree,' he says.

I suddenly realise his are the same eyes that I saw a few nights ago, up on the hill.

'That was you?'

'Yes, and if I wanted you to come to any harm I'd have howled and brought the others. But I didn't want you involved . . .'

'What's changed?'

'Now you are involved. And don't you want to find out more? You won't get many more chances. You've only got a few days left here before you fly back home to Australia. And even if Oberon and Elspeth did come I would protect you. You'd be safe.'

It isn't that Freddie's words are so persuasive that they stop me being scared, but my thirst to learn more about this world is strong and Freddie's words convince me it's safe to go. And that's all they need to do.

'Hold on.' I go back into the room and pull on my coat and boots then return to the balcony.

Freddie jumps down to the roof below and without another thought I climb over the railing and follow him.

I land heavily and for a moment I feel that same confusion as when I awake from sleepwalking. The Mariel that jumped feels like a different person to the one who landed. I straighten up and look back.

'There's only one way back in and that's to follow me,' says Freddie, his eyes glowing red. He runs along the roof and disappears off the end. The next roof we land on slopes and we have to keep moving to avoid falling. There are another couple of easy jumps before we reach a fire escape that takes us down to the ground.

'This is a mistake,' I say. 'I want to go back now.'

Freddie lifts his head to reveal a set of keys hanging around his neck. 'Unless you've got your own set then you have two choices. Come with me or sit here and wait for me to return, hoping that Oberon and Elspeth aren't out tonight.'

He turns his back and walks along the pavement, his tail swishing casually behind him. After a moment's consideration I go after him.

'Come on, we're going this way,' he says.

We go down a dark overgrown path. We step out on

to the canal towpath where the still water reflects the moon. We both stop to look at it. 'How does the moon affect you?' I ask.

'We're most powerful when it's full but as our power grows so does the wolf's voice.'

'What does that mean?'

'When the moon is full, we are more wolf than human. It's when we're most careless. That's why in the stories they say we only change once a month. It's the time we're most likely to get seen.'

'But you don't seem any different to me.'

'Being the wolf doesn't change who you are. Oberon is as greedy a wolf as he is a human, Elspeth was born crazy and I'm just as much fun whatever.'

'So what does the voice say?'

He turns to look at me, the red of his eyes like blood. 'It tells us to *kill kill kill*,' he says. He laughs. 'But don't worry, we can control what we kill. I'm not going to hurt you.'

Freddie stops and sniffs the air. 'There are people up there.'

'I can't see anyone,' I reply.

'I can smell the flesh of two food sources on the water around the next bend so that's either two humans on a boat or two very large ducks.' He grins at me then adds, 'I can't be seen.' He disappears into the undergrowth. 'Don't worry, I'll be right next to you.'

I turn the corner and see a longboat on the canal.

There is light coming from it and two male voices. I feel more vulnerable on my own. The men sound drunk. They are sitting on top of the boat in deck-chairs. There are two pinpricks of light from the cigarettes they're smoking.

I speed up but one of them notices me. 'Hello.'

I keep walking.

'Nice evening for a stroll,' says the other.

I don't look at them as I pass.

'Hey, don't be unfriendly now,' says one. 'Why not stop for a beer?'

Both of them slur their words.

'We only want a little chat.'

Behind me, I hear them both jump off the boat and follow.

'Out late on your lonesome, aren't you?' says one.

'I'm walking my dog. Leave me alone.'

My heart pounds.

One of the men gets in front of me and blocks my way.

The other is behind me. 'What dog?' he says. 'I don't see any dog. Here doggy dog.'

'He's in the bushes,' I say.

The man pulls out a silver lighter, flicks it open, mocking me by pretending to use it to look. Suddenly there's a throaty growl and he flies into the water. Freddie is so fast I barely see him move. There is a second splash as the other man is pushed into the canal.

'Come on,' Freddie whispers.

I run after him. The fear I feel explodes from me as laughter. Freddie allows me to catch up. I see he's holding the man's silver lighter between his jaws.

'What is it about silver?' I ask.

'Silver calls to us,' he replies. 'I don't know why, something about the way it shines in the moonlight. If you were a wolf, your instinct would to be to tear it from me.'

'But aren't you afraid of the others?'

'No, none of the others would dare to attack me.'

'Someone attacked Grandma,' I say.

'Ma'wolf was old. She had grown weak. Even the youngest amongst us could have killed her.'

'Is that who did it? Elspeth?'

'Maybe. She's crazy enough. Or maybe it was Oberon. It could have been any of us. Personally I reckon it was Gerald. I don't think he ever forgave her for coaxing him in the first place.'

'Coaxing,' I repeat. 'What does that mean?'

'It's how we become wolves. The wolf is coaxed out of us with five bites. Gerald was on his own with Ma'wolf for two years before she made him help her coax Oberon, then me and Amelia a year later. We all took part in Lily's coaxing but she refused to bite when Elspeth's turn came.'

'Doesn't it hurt?'

'It hurts a lot at the time, yes. It would kill a human.'

'How old were you when she did it?'

'Wolf children can be coaxed as soon as they can crawl but Grandma waited until each of us was five so we were able to control it.'

'That's terrible.'

'It depends on your point of view. For me, it's an opportunity. How many people get to see a whole other side of life, to run wild at night, to feel the satisfaction of a clean kill?'

I follow Freddie up a path surrounded by trees, making it darker. 'So you don't care who killed Grandma?'

'The pack must protect itself.'

The path takes us to a wire fence, behind which are three small wooden huts, each with a ramp leading up to a tiny door.

'What are they?' I ask.

'Chicken coops.'

'You're going to kill a chicken?' I say, disgusted.

'No. We wait here. You'll see.' Freddie crouches down and I step back into the shadows.

'I still don't understand how the gene is passed down,' I say.

'Well, take me for example. Say I was to have a daughter, she would be a carrier and any of her children would have the gene. But if I had a son, the gene wouldn't be passed on.'

'And would you do that to a little baby? Will you coax Madeleine?'

'Not until she's old enough,' says Freddie. 'But Oberon wants to do it much sooner and we'll have to follow him if he becomes leader.'

'How do you become leader?'

'The wolf with the most kills of the highest value.'

'And is that Oberon?'

'At the moment.' Freddie turns his head. 'Ah look, right on time.'

'Who?'

'Over there.'

A brown fox prowls across the yard. Its eyes are focused on the chicken coops.

'In five seconds time, not-so-Fantastic Mr Fox here is going to break into those huts and slaughter every chicken inside. There are twelve chickens in each hut and Foxy only needs one for tea but he'll kill every single one because killing is in his nature. Providing he can do it before the farmer comes with his shotgun he'll kill three dozen chickens tonight.'

The thought of it horrifies me. 'Can't you scare him away, stop him doing it?' I say.

Freddie winks at me. 'Yep.' He takes two steps back and leaps over the fence. The fox turns to see the source of the noise but Freddie is already upon him. I hear a crunch and a snap before Freddie turns around, holding the limp, lifeless fox between his teeth. He walks back up to the fence and drops the fox at my feet. There's a moment's silence. The chickens have slept through the threat. 'You did it because you wanted to kill,' I say, unable to bring myself to look at the fox.

'Needed to kill,' corrects Freddie. 'Just like Mr Fox, I needed to do it. Unlike him I could control what I killed. I killed one fox efficiently and painlessly and saved thirty-six harmless, innocent chickens.'

16

A Knife in the Hand

When we finally get back to the flat, I go to bed for another night of half sleep. My body feels dirty. I can smell wolf and dead fox on my skin. The smell makes me feel sick. Every time I close my eyes I can see Freddie landing on the fox and I can hear the snap of its neck. I am woken by the sound of Mum's laughter. I get up and dress. I step out of my room to find her and Freddie sitting at the breakfast bar.

'Morning, Mariel,' she says, wiping the tears from her eyes. 'Freddie's been telling me what you got up to last night.'

I catch his eye.

'You should be ashamed of yourself,' says Mum, 'encouraging him to make fun of people like that.'

She is talking about the game in the restaurant. It crosses my mind to tell her the truth, but what would I say? And *did he tell you about turning into a werewolf and killing a fox?* She would think I had lost it. Freddie seems so normal, charming Mum, making her giggle so I smile and pour myself some cereal.

'I told Rob we'd help with the party preparations,' says Mum.

'What party?' I ask.

'We're having a family get-together on the roof. Remember?'

'Won't that be cold?' I say.

'Outdoor heaters,' says Freddie. 'There's a sound system up there too.'

Mum says, 'It'll be nice to see the whole family again before we return home, won't it, Mariel?'

I don't reply.

'Can you believe it's been a week since the funeral?' asks Uncle Robson.

'Is it Monday already?' says Mum. 'Doesn't school start today?'

'It's an INSET day,' says Freddie.

Uncle Robson nods and says, 'Yes, but you do have homework that needs doing for tomorrow.'

'I need to entertain Mariel!' protests Freddie.

'I'm sure Mariel can keep herself entertained,' says Uncle Robson firmly.

'Can I email my friends?' I ask. 'I said I'd tell them what it's like in England.'

'Sure. You can use my study,' says Uncle Robson.

The study and computer are state of the art just like the

rest of the flat. I sit down on the plush swivel chair and log into my email account. There are two emails from friends. Reading what they have been up to makes me feel homesick. I look out of the window at the cold English sky. Both my friends want to know how it is here. I hit the reply button and sit staring at the blinking cursor wondering what to say. But I feel so detached from my life back home that it's like I don't even know how to write to my friends so I click away from the email and find a search engine instead. I type in 'cycles of the moon' and find a calendar showing the shape of the moon each night. I look up the date Grandma's body was found. The night before it shows a perfect circle. Grandma died on the night the moon was full and when my cousins were strongest and wildest. I close the page, delete my search history and go to the kitchen to help Mum.

Freddie's in his room doing his homework and Uncle Robson is out buying stuff for the party so it's just the two of us.

'What do you think about moving back to England for good?' she says out of the blue.

'Australia's our home,' I say.

She ignores this. 'I'd get a job and you could start school here. We'll arrange it at the beginning of the next school year. That way it won't be so disruptive.'

'Moving to the other side of the world, away from my life, away from my friends. Isn't that exactly what disruptive means?'

'You'll make new friends.' Mum is concentrating on the pastry she is flattening, avoiding eye contact.

'I don't want to move,' I say.

'You've enjoyed getting to know your cousins, haven't you?'

'My cousins are . . .'

'They're what, Mariel?'

'They're not normal,' I whisper in case Freddie can hear from his room.

'Oh, for goodness' sake. I thought we dealt with all this.'

'*Dealt* with it?' I exclaim. 'No, we didn't deal with it. We never deal with anything. Were you ever going to tell me about how Grandad died?'

Mum stops what she's doing. She looks like she is about to cry, but I don't want her to cry because every time she does it means it's the end of the conversation and this is something we need to talk about.

'Who told you?' she asks.

'It doesn't matter. Why didn't you tell me?'

'He was terrified of her. Then suddenly he died like that. What was I to think? And how could I explain any of it to you?'

'You don't understand anything,' I say.

'Mariel, what are you doing with that knife?'

I look down and see that I am clutching a bread knife. I must have pulled it out of the washing-up bowl but to Mum it looks like I am threatening her with it. I put the knife down.

'I'm getting worried about you,' she says quietly.

Suddenly I need to get away from her. I turn to leave.

'Mariel, where are you going? Your cousins will be here soon.'

'I'm going out,' I say. 'You can clean up your own mess.'

I step on to the pavement outside Uncle Robson's place wishing I could be transported home. I want to be as far from Mum as possible. I turn corner after corner, looking down, barely noticing the people and buildings I pass. I want to lose myself in these streets. I want to disappear. My mind plays out imagined conversations with Mum, none of which end well, even though I'm doing both parts. The rhythm of my feet helps calm me and focus my thoughts. Was it a coincidence that I picked up the kitchen knife or did I reach for it? I would never harm Mum. I know that. So why do I repeat this in my head as though I need convincing that it's true?

I have no idea where I am. There are no shops or schools here. Just offices and businesses. Nothing looks familiar. I look behind me and wonder how I will be able to find my way back. I can't even remember the last turn I made. A couple of men in suits walk past, talking seriously. A jogger runs the other way, huffing and puffing. I could ask someone for directions but I don't even know what road Uncle Robson lives on.

I sit on a wall and wonder what to do. I want to go back. Not just home to Melbourne but back to before I knew what I know. I want my old life back, where I only have to worry about normal things, like school-work and friendships and boys.

'Need a lift?'

I look up and see Uncle Will leaning out of a car window. Aunt Chrissie is sitting next to him at the steering wheel and there's a baby-seat in the back with Madeleine in it.

'I got lost,' I say, relieved to see them.

'This part of Chilton is a bit of a maze. Hop in. We're on our way to the party.'

I climb into the back seat next to Madeleine, who looks at me and gurgles.

'You're lucky we're running late,' says Aunt Chrissie. She smiles at me in the rear-view mirror. 'Mind you, we're always running late now we have this little one.'

I offer Madeleine my finger. She grips it tightly. Aunt Chrissie starts the car.

'Are you enjoying your stay with the flash uncle then?' asks Will.

'It's a great place,' I reply.

'Well, don't get used to all that luxury. You're coming to stay with us next.'

'Do you live in Chilton too?'

'Yes, we rent an apartment on the cheap side of town, near the university.' He smiles at Aunt Chrissie.

They both seem a lot younger than my other aunts and uncles. I look at Madeleine, clutching my finger and staring at me with her big blue eyes. She's a Considine. She is the child of a son. It is difficult to believe it but there is a wolf inside her, waiting to be awakened. I recall the picture of Grandma looking at her so fondly, anticipating the day she can make her one of the pack. What will happen to her now? Will the others coax the wolf out in her when she's old enough? Is she destined to become one of them? Looking at this sweet little baby it's difficult to imagine that she could ever lose her innocence, let alone transform into a hideous creature.

'Will you stay living near the rest of the family now Grandma's gone?' I ask.

'I don't know,' replies Uncle Will. 'Now we have the money from the will it might be time to move somewhere else.'

'Yes, you should move away,' I say, aware of how odd this must sound.

'Chilton's charms haven't won you over then?'

'No, I mean you should live wherever you want to now.'

'Thank you.'

They share a puzzled look, which I pretend not to notice.

17

SHATTERING ICE

The lift takes us to the top floor, then we go up some stairs. There are party sounds coming from above on the roof terrace. It is a cold day but outdoor heaters are blasting out heat. Everyone is gathered there. Mum spots me and waves but doesn't make any effort to come over and talk to me. My uncles are standing next to a bar, except for Uncle Robson who is showing Aunt Ruth some of the features of the roof. Will takes photos of everyone. Aunt Dee is talking to Aunt Celeste. My six cousins are standing together, away from their parents, deep in conversation. It reminds me of the first time I saw them, standing outside the church. Just like that day Gerald spots me first and alerts the others to my arrival.

They turn to face me. My instinct is to run but I don't move. Amelia dashes over to hug me. Her perfume is so strong it feels like it is burning my nostril hairs. The others reform the circle without her.

'It's so good to see you. I've missed you being around. What have you been up to? Isn't Rob's place amazing? I love the view you get up here.' She speaks quickly. 'Oh, and guess what? I got the part.'

'The "Wow, that's fresh" part?' I ask.

'Yes, they said I was the best person for the role. We're filming next week. I've been practising a new emphasis. Listen. W*ow*, that's *fresh*.'

It sounds no different to me but I smile and say, 'It's perfect.'

Amelia's enthusiasm is overwhelming but I can't bring myself to say anything else.

'Have you seen they've even got a bar here? Imagine what this place will be like in the summer. I mean, these outdoor heaters work really well but it'll be lovely when you can sunbathe up here. Freddie says they're going to have parties all through the summer. It's such a shame you won't be around but . . .'

'Amelia,' I interrupt. 'I can't.'

'Can't what?'

'I can't talk like this now I know about you.'

She laughs uncomfortably. 'Let's not go on about all that now. Let's have a proper catch-up. How did you like the university? I'll probably go there after my A-levels. They've got an excellent drama course. I've decided to give acting another try now.'

'I can't pretend everything is fine and normal when it's not.'

'Not so near the others,' she whispers. She leads me to a corner of the roof. 'All right, so you know the truth. What of it? It doesn't change anything.' Her tone is different. She sounds more serious, angry even.

'You change,' I reply.

'Only at night. We're no different in the daytime.'

'We're not talking about what colour pyjamas you wear. You're a wolf. You're a killer. You all are.'

Amelia throws me a dark look. 'It's just a genetic thing.'

'Like the smell?' I don't say it to be cruel but it sounds terrible when I hear it come out of my mouth. 'I'm sorry,' I say quickly.

'Yes, like that. Grandma said my condition happens sometimes when two strands combine. I suppose somewhere in Mum's history someone must have had that too. I just wish it hadn't happened to me. If it had been Oberon, no one would even notice, he smells so awful anyway. But that's just because he doesn't wash.'

In spite of everything I laugh at this. 'Do you like being a wolf?' I ask.

'It's difficult to explain.' Amelia looks down and speaks softly. 'When you're the wolf, no one judges you. No one tells you what to do. No one tells you you're not pretty enough or that your hair is the wrong colour or you're too short or too tall or too fat or too skinny. No one tells you you're too anything. You just are.'

'But you are pretty and slim and you have nice hair. I don't understand. You just got that part, didn't you?'

She looks directly at me for the first time. 'Mum called the casting company and explained about my condition and how if I didn't get the role because of the smell she would sue them for discrimination. That's why they offered me the part.'

'But all those amazing pictures you showed me?'

'Every single part I go up for I'm up against girls who are just as pretty but who don't have to drown themselves in perfume every ten minutes. It's not like that when I'm the wolf. I can do whatever I want.'

I feel sorry for Amelia but I can't get the sound of the fox's neck snapping out of my head. 'You don't get judged as wolves because you don't get caught. But every night you go out and murder some poor creature.'

'It's in our nature,' she replies.

'What about Grandma? Whose nature was it in to kill her?'

'Grandma tripped . . .'

'And fell down the stairs,' I say. 'Yes, I know the story but I don't believe it. She died during a full moon, when you were all strong and out of control. One of you killed her.'

'Well, it wasn't me.'

'Who was it then?'

'What does it matter?'

'It matters because it's murder.'

'People have lots of words like murder and execution and assassination. For wolves, a kill is a kill. We shouldn't be talking about this.'

'Who killed Grandma? Was it Elspeth?'

'Elspeth was Grandma's favourite.' She glances over at the others. 'You should stay out of this. Soon you'll go back home to your normal life. You're lucky.'

'And what about Madeleine? Is she lucky? Will you all leave her alone or will you drag her into this world of yours?'

'Madeleine is a Considine.'

'What does that mean?'

'Please. It doesn't matter.' Amelia stands up. 'You should forget all of this. Let's go and join the rest of the party.'

'Mariel is enjoying herself. Aren't you, cuz?' Oberon joins us. He has his hands in his pockets and a dark threatening look in his eyes.

'Smile please,' says Uncle Will, appearing with his camera.

Oberon grins and Amelia pouts but I can't bring myself to pretend.

Will takes the photo. The flash leaves stars in my eyes.

Mum joins us. 'Mariel,' she says, 'would you give me a hand? I need to bring some champagne up. We're going to have a toast.'

'Hi, Auntie Lynda,' says Oberon. 'Mariel and me have got some catching up to do. Would it be all right if Amelia were to help you instead?'

'Well, I suppose. Is that OK with you, Amelia?' she asks.

Amelia looks at me. 'Of course. I'd love to help,' she replies.

Mum and Amelia go downstairs and Oberon turns to me. 'You were lucky the other night. Lily has a weakness for the weak. She holds too much fear in her heart, just like my brother.' His sweaty face is much nearer to mine than I would like. 'They're scared of the wolf's voice. They don't embrace it like I do, like Grandma did. Wolves shouldn't know fear.'

'Not even fear of people finding out?'

Oberon chuckles. 'Who's going to tell? You?'

'If you keep falling asleep in cowsheds, I won't have to tell anyone. Someone is bound to get proof soon enough.'

'I suppose you mean your friend in the dog collar?' says Oberon. He laughs, seeing the look on my face. 'You thought we didn't know? Grandma protected the silly old fool. She stopped us from hunting him down in the woods like he deserves but she's not around to stop us any more. Next time he goes out at night looking for proof I'll tear off his dog collar and rip out his throat.'

Oberon is leaning forward, whispering this in my

ear. His words have a strange effect on me. I am rooted to the spot with fear. Over his shoulder, the family gathering looks like the most ordinary thing in the world.

'Did you kill Grandma?' I ask.

'What do you think?' he says with a smile. 'Besides, it was her who taught us there's no such thing as a bad kill. What do you care anyway? You were dead to her long before she died. She only cared about wolves. Our parents were just carriers of the gene. Your mother was nothing to her and you were less than nothing.'

He walks away. In the other corner Aunt Chrissie is cuddling Madeleine, gently rocking her and singing in her ear.

I head towards the food but Elspeth intercepts me. 'I do hope you're going to come out to play tonight,' she says.

'What's your problem with me?'

Elspeth stands closer than I'd like. 'The first bite for the blood to appear, the second for the pain and for the tears, the third and fourth cause anger and fear. The fifth must be felt for the wolf to be here.'

'That's about coaxing, isn't it? Five bites to coax out the wolf.'

She grins. 'With each sun that rises and sets, the pack goes from two legs to four, but feast upon flesh of your own and you will change no more.'

'What does that mean? Why would you want to change no more?'

'Never fight a wolf in the moonlight, your fingernails will meet with claws, your fear with death then your final breath draws as your red blood pours.'

'Lovely,' I reply. 'Do you know *The Owl and the Pussycat*?'

The sound of tinkling glasses makes everyone go quiet. Uncle Robson pulls out a remote control from his pocket and turns the music off. Everyone has a glass of champagne. Amelia brings two glasses of grape juice for Elspeth and me.

'Your mum's going to make a speech,' she says.

'Thank you, everyone,' Mum begins. 'When Mariel and I flew over last week, neither of us knew what to expect. I hadn't seen you all for over a decade. Some of you I had never met at all. Some of you hadn't been born.' Madeleine makes a funny squeaking noise that makes everyone laugh. 'But you have all been so welcoming, we can't thank you enough.'

My uncles cheer and everyone raises their glasses.

'And because you have all been so wonderful, Mariel and I have decided that we're going to move back to England.' She catches my eye. 'We're coming home.'

Aunt Celeste is the first to hug Mum. Uncle Robson says, 'That's terrific news.' Everyone else clinks glasses. Will's camera flashes. Amelia throws her arms around me, causing me to spill most of my drink. Freddie gives me a thumbs-up. Lily and Gerald cast dark glances at me.

'And I was about to announce that we're moving to Australia,' says Uncle Will.

Everyone laughs again.

'While we've got your attention, we've got an announcement too,' says Oberon. 'As you know, when Grandma died she left the house to us, her beloved grandchildren.' I wonder if his sarcasm is as obvious to the others. 'Well, we've just been discussing it and we've decided that we'd like it to be used by someone who really needs it, the youngest of the Considine cousins, little Madsie. Uncle Will and Aunt Chrissie, we'd like you to have Louvre House.'

Everyone looks touched by the speech. Uncle Harkett and Aunt Ruth smile proudly. More wine is poured. There are more hugs and kisses, more congratulations from uncles.

My head is swimming. The sickened look on Gerald's face as he is congratulated makes me realise what they have done. They did it for Madeleine. They heard Will and Chrissie talking about moving away and did this to keep Madeleine nearby. I need to talk to Mum.

She is standing next to Aunt Chrissie, holding Madeleine. I walk over to her, passing Aunt Dee who is saying to Aunt Celeste, 'That sounds terrible. How many did they kill?'

'Two. A mare and a foal. The police think it's some-one's idea of a prank after all these ridiculous stories about the beast of Wilderdale.'

'Slaughtering horses, not exactly my idea of a joke.'

Mum is blowing raspberries on Madeleine's cheeks, making her giggle. 'I've been trying to work out whether she looks more like you or Will,' she says.

'I think she's getting too hot under these heaters,' Aunt Chrissie replies, taking her daughter off Mum.

'Mum, can we talk?' I ask.

'Here we go, I told you I'd be in trouble.' She winks at Aunt Chrissie.

'Have you had a nice stay, Mariel?' asks Aunt Chrissie diplomatically.

'Very nice,' I lie.

'I'm so pleased you've decided to come back.'

'We haven't,' I say.

Aunt Chrissie looks unsure what to say to this response but I don't really want to talk to her about it.

'Mum,' I say, forcefully, 'we need to talk.'

'Can't you just enjoy yourself, Mariel? We'll discuss it later. This is a party. Look, your cousins are all enjoying themselves. Why can't you be a bit more like them?'

They are on the other side of the roof, leaning over the edge, cheering every so often. Mum continues her conversation with Aunt Chrissie. This infuriates me but I can see I'm getting nowhere so I go to join my cousins. They have all hitched themselves up on their elbows, where the roof overlooks the street. I take a place next to Lily at the end of the line.

'What are you doing?' I ask.

'The heaters are weakening the icicles,' she replies.

Below the ledge is a clump of ice from a broken pipe. A row of icicles has formed. Freddie is using a stick to bang the roof just above the icicles.

'Look, one's about to go,' says Freddie. The vibration from the stick causes the icicle to drop. It catches the light before hitting the pavement and shattering.

I don't join in the cheer but it is pretty amazing to watch.

'Who's next with the stick?' asks Freddie.

'It's my turn,' replies Oberon, grabbing it off him and tapping above the biggest icicle.

'Choose a different one. That one will take ages to go,' says Freddie.

'It'll make the biggest crash though,' replies Oberon.

Gerald says, 'Wait, there are people coming.' I notice a couple walking arm in arm.

Oberon leans further over, so he can reach the icicle itself with the stick. The couple are still approaching, unaware of the danger above.

'Oberon, stop it,' says Gerald.

Oberon looks at him resentfully. 'You don't get to tell me what to do, bro.'

'Come on, Obe, we don't want anyone to get hurt,' reasons Freddie.

With another direct whack Oberon chips a piece of ice from the top, making the icicle wobble precariously.

'You could kill them,' I say.

Elspeth says, 'It wouldn't count though.'

Oberon simply laughs and hits it one more time, finally dislodging the huge chunk of ice.

'Look out,' I scream. The couple stop and look around them, trying to figure out where the voice came from. There is silence while we watch the ice fall. The couple leap back and the woman screams as it smashes into pieces on the pavement right in front of them. It misses them by centimetres. We all move away from the edge, out of sight.

18

MR PICKLES HAS A NASTY FRIGHT

Will and Chrissie are the first to leave the party because Madeleine has started grizzling. Sewell and Dee are next. Aunt Dee tells Lily and Elspeth to say goodbye to me because we won't see each other again before Mum and I fly back home.

Elspeth addresses me in her usual threatening hiss. 'Avoid dark passages and shady lanes, or feel as my claws rip the blood from your veins.'

'You should write greetings cards when you're older,' I say. 'You have quite a talent.'

Lily doesn't say anything more than a simple goodbye.

'I want the diary back,' I say.

'No,' she whispers.

'I found it,' I say.

'No.' Lily glares at me. There is fear in her eyes. 'This isn't a game. You need to persuade your mum not to move back.'

'Believe me, I'm trying.'

Amelia, when it's her turn to leave, flings her arms around me dramatically. 'I can't believe you're going. You'll be back though, won't you? I'll email you a link to my advert when it's made. I'm going up for a part in the school play next. It should be really good experience. Lots of actors learn their trade in theatre.'

'Goodbye, Amelia,' I reply, hugging her.

Harkett and Ruth stay longest talking to Uncle Robson and Mum.

Gerald and I find ourselves standing together, apart from the others. I haven't spoken to him since the last night at his house. Could Freddie be right that it was him who killed Grandma? Standing in the corner of the party, nervously avoiding everyone else, he doesn't look like he could kill anything.

'Freddie said you were the first to be coaxed,' I say.

'He shouldn't have told you. You shouldn't want to know any more about us.' He glances around, checking no one is listening.

'I want to protect Madeleine,' I say.

'You can't protect her. She's a Considine.'

Mum laughs loudly at something Uncle Harkett is saying.

Oberon, who has run out of spare food to hoover up,

says, 'Come on, Dad, it's time to go. Some of us need to get our beauty sleep.'

'Quite right, darling. Come on, Harkett,' says Aunt Ruth.

After they have said their goodbyes, Uncle Robson, Freddie, Mum and I go downstairs. I still want to talk to Mum but she's tipsy and giggly so I go to bed. I don't want to see Freddie but he is waiting for me when I come out of the bathroom.

'I'll knock for you when they've gone to bed,' he says.

'I'm not going out again,' I reply.

'Why? Last night was fun, wasn't it?'

'I don't want to be a part of this. I wish I didn't know.' I try to push past him but he blocks my way.

'You'll be completely safe.'

'With each sun that rises and sets, the pack goes from two legs to four, but feast upon flesh of your own and you will change no more,' I say, repeating the poem that has been stuck in my head since Elspeth said it.

'You don't want to worry about that stuff,' says Freddie casually.

'It means that if you kill and eat me, you won't have to change into wolves, doesn't it?'

'No, it doesn't mean that. It's about how we go full wolf.'

'Full wolf?'

'Some packs grow tired of their double lives, so their leader takes them to completion. They choose to stay as wolves for ever.'

'How?'

'The pack must perform a ritual that begins with the eating of another wolf. You aren't a wolf so eating you wouldn't count.'

'Oberon and Elspeth still tried to kill me.'

'That was different. That was just about the leadership. Neither of them would dare touch you while you're with me. Besides, after those horses, Oberon has enough kills to walk into the leadership. He doesn't need you. Come out tonight and we'll have some fun.'

'No.'

I go to my room. Later that night he taps on my window but I don't move from my bed. I can see his muscular wolf-shaped shadow on the curtain. I am torn in two. I am consumed by an urge to go but fear binds me to the bed. When he eventually gives up, I am both relieved and disappointed. I sleep soundly and dreamlessly but wake the next morning groggy and tired.

Freddie has gone to school when I get up and Uncle Robson is on an important business call so Mum and I head over to Will and Chrissie's flat in the hire car.

I am grateful there are no cousins at Will and

Chrissie's to intimidate me or freak me out. Only Madeleine lying on her back wearing a white sleep-suit, waving her arms and legs in the air. The flat is above a chip shop and I can instantly see why they want to move to Louvre House. It might be old and creepy but at least there is space and it doesn't smell of chip fat. Their flat is made even more cramped by the stacks of framed photographs everywhere. The back room is Uncle Will's studio with a big light on a stand and a brown textured background I recognise from some of the portrait photos of Amelia.

'Sorry the place is such a tip,' says Will. 'We're in a bit of chaos because of the exhibition tomorrow.'

Aunt Chrissie laughs. 'Don't believe a word of it. It's always like this.'

'What exhibition?' I ask.

'Of my art,' says Will. 'It's tomorrow. There are lots of important people coming. I might even sell something if Robson brings some of his friends who have more money than sense.'

We all sit down in the living room. Madeleine has grabbed hold of her feet and rocks back and forward until she rolls on to her side. I go to help her but Aunt Chrissie stops me.

'Let her try herself. I think she's going to start crawling any day now.'

Madeleine rolls over on to her tummy and waves her arms and legs around but isn't able to propel herself forwards. I feel sick and helpless at the thought of her being bitten by wolves. Why can't they leave her alone?

'The problem is she hasn't got anywhere to go in this flat,' says Aunt Chrissie.

'You should come to Australia with us. There are lots of big houses there,' I say.

Will, Chrissie and Mum laugh.

'I think you've forgotten that we're moving here,' says Mum.

'We could swap places. We'll come and live here, you stay in our place in Melbourne.'

'I couldn't go back to Louvre House,' says Mum.

'I know what you mean,' replies Aunt Chrissie.

'Come on,' says Will. 'If we move into Mum's old place, we can use some of that money to do it up. We could even afford a holiday. Remember those?'

'It's just so isolated,' says Aunt Chrissie.

Uncle Will sighs, exasperated. 'I know it's a bit of a spooky old place but we wouldn't be paying rent. Let's face it, my photography only just keeps us afloat.'

Aunt Chrissie says, 'I'd feel like she was looking down on me, judging. It was always me she blamed for failing to give her a grandchild.'

'You gave her Madeleine,' I say.

Aunt Chrissie picks up Madeleine and stands her up. She pulls a funny face which makes Madeleine giggle. 'Do you know what Flora did when she came to the hospital to visit her the first time?'

'Oh, come on, this isn't fair,' says Will.

Aunt Chrissie ignores him. 'She snatched her out of my arms. It was like I wasn't even there.'

'She thought you were handing her over,' he says.

'She thought no such thing,' she replies.

The doorbell goes and Will remembers he has a customer.

I hear a familiar dog bark before I see that his customer is the organist from the church.

'More pictures of Mr Pickles, Mrs Mills?' says Aunt Chrissie.

'Poor Mr Pickles isn't quite himself today,' replies Mrs Mills feeding him a biscuit. 'So this is a special treat to cheer him up, isn't it, Mr Pickles?'

'He does seem a bit subdued,' says Uncle Will, raising an eyebrow at me.

'Something gave him a terrible fright in the garden last night. He's not the only one either. I've heard all sorts of stories about pets being attacked or going missing . . . And what about Farmer Dooley's cow and those horses? The papers are saying it's the beast of Wilderdale. It must be as old as me if so because people have been talking about it since I was a little girl. Poor Mr Pickles.'

'Well, let's try some photographic therapy, shall we?' says Will, closing the door behind them.

Aunt Chrissie whispers, 'It's the third time this year she's been. How many photos of the dog does she need?'

'Aren't you worried about all these attacks at night?' I say. 'This isn't the right place to bring up Madeleine.'

'What on earth are you talking about?" asks Mum.

'I just mean that something killed that cow and those horses and scared Mr Pickles.'

'Every so often these rumours appear,' says Aunt Chrissie. 'And the papers love putting two and two together to make five. That reminds me. Ruth said Farmer Dooley thought Oberon had something to do with the cow.'

'He has got a big appetite, but a whole cow?' adds Mum.

They both laugh at the joke. 'Right, a cup of tea, I think.' Aunt Chrissie gets up.

'I'll help you,' says Mum.

'Mariel, you're on Madeleine watch,' says Chrissie. 'I'm terrified that the first thing she'll do when she crawls is head straight for one of the big frames and get flattened by her father's art.'

Madeleine waves her arms around excitedly.

There is a hatch through to the kitchen so I can still hear Mum and Aunt Chrissie's conversation.

'Do you think you will move to Louvre House then?' asks Mum.

'Probably. Will's right. It makes sense really. Besides, she's dead now. She can't hurt me any more. Sorry to speak ill of your mum, Lynda.'

'Don't you worry. She was always horrible to me. It

was women, I think. Maybe she felt threatened by them. I'm surprised Dee hasn't written an entire book on her.'

The rest of the day is spent indoors. Sleet falls, washing away what's left of the snow and creating rivers of grey sludge that run along the side of the road.

'It's such a shame about the weather,' says Aunt Chrissie. 'There are some nice walks on this side of town up into the hills.'

Once Mrs Mills has gone, Will lets me use his digital camera and I take loads of pictures of Madeleine. In the evening Aunt Chrissie makes pasta.

'Now I should warn you that we're vegetarians,' she says.

'Me too,' I say.

'What about Madeleine?' asks Mum.

'She does look tasty but I don't think we should eat her,' jokes Aunt Chrissie.

Everyone laughs at the joke but I don't find it funny.

'We haven't decided what to do about her yet. It should probably be her choice and all the books say you shouldn't dissuade them from eating anything to start with.'

Mum says, 'That's true. This one used to love chicken.'

'Until I found out what I was eating,' I reply.

Over dinner Will says, 'I'm sorry we're not taking you out to eat but we have a few financial issues until Mum's money comes through.'

'Don't worry about it,' replies Mum. 'This is all lovely. We're quite happy.'

Because Will and Chrissie's flat is so small and because Madeleine needs a room of her own in order to sleep through the night, Mum and I share a sofa bed in the studio. During the night I wake up twice. The first time because Madeleine is crying. When she goes quiet, I fall straight back to sleep and for the first time in my life I dream.

It is every bit as strange as I imagined it would be. In it I relive the night I went out with Freddie, except I see it through Freddie's eyes. I see myself walking by the canal. I see the glint of the man's silver lighter and feel the urge to snatch it. I experience the surge of power as I push the men into the canal, then the satisfaction of catching the fox, but as I land on its back my point of view changes to that of the fox. My body aches under Freddie's weight. I feel wordless panic and instinctive fear. I scrabble to get free but he overpowers me. I know I am about to die. I feel the snap in my neck and I awake to a voice saying, 'Mariel, what are you doing?'

The voice isn't part of the dream.

I wake up. It's Mum.

'You're causing a draught. Close the window,' she says irritably.

I'm standing up. I have walked to the window and opened it.

19

HOLES

The next morning we sit in the living room, playing with Madeleine. Will pokes his head through the hatch between the kitchen and the living room, making her laugh, and says, 'What do you want to do with your last day?'

'We're happy to fall in with your plans,' says Mum, answering for both of us.

'As long as it doesn't involve being outside,' I add, looking out at the street below, which has all but vanished behind a mist of drizzle.

Will ducks down and reappears for Madeleine's benefit. 'I've got to go and put the finishing touches to the exhibition if you want to come to the gallery with me.'

'Sounds lovely,' says Mum.

On the way to the gallery Will teases Mum about her driving.

'I suppose you are used to driving on the other side of the road,' he says, grinning.

'We drive on the same side in Australia,' she replies.

'What, the middle?'

'At least I can drive,' she responds.

'That's debatable,' he says.

The two of them laugh and I don't find it hard to imagine what they were like as children. He is the closest in age to her of all my uncles. I want to join in with them but I am feeling strangely distanced from everything.

Mum parks outside the gallery and we step out. We go through a door and up some stairs to the gallery where Will's pictures are hanging in a white-walled room. He is carrying two last minute additions. 'See if you can guess the theme,' he says.

There are photographs of walls, trees, people and animals. There are everyday objects and ones I can't quite make out. Some are in colour, others in black and white. There is a hole in a wall, a knot in a tree trunk, an open mouth, a rabbit caught mid-run towards its burrow.

'I give up,' I say.

'Every picture has a hole at its centre,' explains Will. 'Some are more obvious than others.'

Now he says it I can see that each one is carefully composed to put the hole at the dead centre of the photograph. It's really clever but Mum looks doubtful and says, 'Holes, Will?'

'Everywhere you go you see holes. Manholes,

buttonholes, holes in walls, in the ground. But they all serve a purpose and they all tell us something about ourselves as a society,' he replies.

'Holes?' she says.

They both laugh.

'All right, so it is a bit pretentious but critics like a theme,' he says.

I say, 'I think they're brilliant. This one's great.'

I'm standing in front of a picture taken from underneath a picnic table, looking up. You can see blue sky in between the wooden slats, with a circle where the umbrella would slot in.

'And you took them all?' I ask.

'All except this one.'

Will indicates the picture next to it. It is an old, tattered black-and-white photo of Grandma's house. The photo has so many rips it looks like it would fall apart if it wasn't for the frame. Its edges are rough and in its centre the front door to the house is open.

'It's Louvre House,' I say, looking closely at the picture.

'Yes, I found that when we were tidying up Mum's stuff. Look carefully and you can see your grandad as a boy in the bottom right window.'

Getting up close, I see a pale white face behind the glass.

'So the house belonged to Grandad's side of the family,' I say.

'Oh yes, his side had the money,' says Mum. 'Dad used to joke Mum only married him for his money.'

Will bangs a nail into a wall and hangs one of the pictures he has brought with him. 'This is one of my most recent ones.'

It's a photo of Madeleine's right eye. Her pupil is a black droplet in a circle of blue.

'I wonder if her eyes will change colour,' says Mum.

'I don't think they'll change now,' replies Will. 'She has Chrissie's eyes.'

'You never know. Those Considine genes are pretty strong.'

'Not in Madeleine, they're not.' He smiles and it's clear he has more to say. He checks the picture is straight then says, 'The thing is, Chrissie didn't want anyone to know but I can't see any point in hiding it now. After all, we only kept it secret in the first place because of Mum. Now she's gone I'm not embarrassed about it. I'd rather everyone knew the truth. In fact I think the whole thing is miraculous.' He pauses, then says, 'Madeleine isn't mine. I wasn't able to have children.'

'Who's her father?' asks Mum.

'Me in every sense but biological.'

'But whose . . .' Mum glances at me, apparently unsure how much detail she should go into in front of me.

'A donor,' replies Will.

But I don't care about how. All that matters is that Madeleine isn't one of them. She can't be coaxed. She can grow up to live a normal life.

'And you haven't told anyone?' says Mum.

'Not until now. You know how funny Mum could be, so we kept it from her. Now she's gone though, I'd rather come out in the open about it but Chrissie is less sure.'

'Yes, you need to tell the rest of the family,' I say.

'It's more complicated than that, Mariel,' says Mum in a patronising tone.

Mum has no idea how complicated it really is. If the others don't know the truth, they will still try to coax her when she's old enough and end up killing her. If they know she isn't a Considine, they will leave her alone.

'Chrissie's scared they won't think of her as family. Her cousins absolutely dote on her at the moment,' says Will.

He bangs a nail into the wall and hangs the other picture he has brought with him. It is of him and Chrissie standing in front of a brick wall, hand in hand. Neither of them is smiling. There is something about the picture which makes me feel sad.

'I can't see the hole in this one,' I say.

'That was taken before we had Madeleine,' replies Will.

20
THE WOLF MOON

Back at the flat, the first thing I do is give Madeleine a big cuddle. She dribbles on my shoulder but I don't care. She isn't one of them. She cannot be coaxed.

We stay in for the rest of the day. Will is clearly nervous about the show and grows more and more nervous throughout the afternoon. His tetchiness is made worse when Madeleine is sick on Chrissie's dress just as we are supposed to be leaving.

'I'd better change. It'll only take a minute,' says Chrissie.

'It took you three hours to pick that one out,' snaps Will.

His mood worsens when he gets a call from Uncle Harkett to say they are running late.

'Why doesn't Mum drive us there instead?' I suggest.

'We have to wait for them. Oberon and Gerald are babysitting for Madeleine,' says Chrissie.

My heart quickens. This is my last night in England and I was looking forward to going to Will's exhibition, but I can't go out and leave Madeleine with Oberon and Gerald. I feel sick because I know what I have to do. I must stay behind and talk to my cousins, tell them the truth about Madeleine.

'I've been thinking,' I say. 'Since I've seen the exhibition this morning I'm more than happy to stay in and babysit tonight too if you'd like.'

'Don't you want to come along and big me up?' Will sounds disappointed. 'One day I may actually sell a picture.'

'I'm sure Mariel would rather spend the evening with people her own age, Will,' Chrissie says.

The buzzer goes.

'That will be the boys.' Uncle Will stomps down the stairs to answer the door.

I hear Oberon's voice say, 'Mum and Dad are waiting in the car.'

When Oberon swaggers in, I am holding Madeleine up on her feet, bouncing her up and down.

'Ah, ickle Cousin Madsie and ickle Cousin Mariel. Hello,' says Oberon. He grabs the remote control and switches the TV on. 'There'd better be some meat in the fridge. I'm starving. Maybe I'll go with the vegetarian option.' He laughs at his joke, then shrugs. 'Suit yourself.' He goes to the kitchen, barging past Gerald coming the other way.

'I'm staying with Madeleine,' I say.

'You should go to the exhibition with your mum,' says Gerald. 'It's not safe for you here.'

Aunt Chrissie dashes in, kisses Madeleine goodbye and reminds Gerald he has her mobile number if he should need it. She doesn't seem at all worried about leaving her baby with them. But why would she? She doesn't know the truth.

'Keep an eye on her,' says Chrissie. 'She actually managed to crawl for the first time this afternoon.'

'That's great news,' says Oberon from the kitchen.

'Chrissie, come on,' shouts Will.

'Sorry!' Chrissie kisses Madeleine again and leaves. They are in such a hurry that Mum forgets to say goodbye until she's at the bottom of the stairs. 'Oh, bye, Mariel, see you later,' she shouts up as an afterthought.

'Bye, Mum,' I respond too quietly for her to hear.

Oberon comes back into the room, bends down and talks to Madeleine. 'Crawling, eh, little wolf? That means you can be coaxy-woaxed now.'

'She's too young,' replies Gerald.

'Not for what I have in mind,' snarls Oberon.

A look of horror crosses Gerald's face. 'I won't do it. Nor will the others.'

Oberon stands up to face his brother and snarls, 'Tonight when I become pack leader you'll all do as I say.'

'Not that.'

174

'Madeleine can't be coaxed,' I say. 'She isn't one of you. Will isn't her real father.'

'That's just a pathetic attempt to save her,' says Oberon. 'I'd spend more time protecting yourself and less time worrying about ickle wickle Madsie, if I were you.'

'I don't care what you do to me. Leave Madeleine alone,' I say. I pick her up but take her by surprise and she starts to bawl. I try to comfort her but she thrashes around, pounding me with her fists.

'Now, don't tell me that's not a Considine,' says Oberon.

Gerald takes her from me and she instantly calms down.

'If you don't believe me, call Chrissie and ask her,' I say.

'Yeah, Gerald,' says Oberon. 'Why don't you call Chrissie and ask her who Madsie's daddy is. I'll put her to bed.' Oberon takes Madeleine from his brother. 'You ready for bed, ickle Madsie?' he asks her. 'Oh, she's definitely one of us. I can see the wolf in her eyes.'

Oberon leaves the room. Gerald pulls out a mobile phone.

'Will isn't her father,' I whisper. 'He can't have children. He told us today.'

Gerald finds Chrissie's number but doesn't call it.

'Gerald, you have to believe me,' I say desperately.

'This is the truth?' he says.

I nod. 'Will said they are going to tell everyone now Grandma's gone.'

Gerald puts his phone away.

'You're not going to call?'

'Tonight is Uncle Will's big night. I don't want to ruin that.'

'But Madeleine.'

'Don't worry, if she's not related to us she's in no danger. We won't let him coax her.'

There's a crashing noise from the back room. Gerald looks at me. He doesn't need to say anything; I understand the look of fear in his eyes.

'Obe?' he shouts.

We run to Madeleine's room to find the curtain flapping in the wind. Both Oberon and Madeleine are gone.

'Where's he taken her?' I ask. I remember Elspeth's poem. *With each sun that rises and sets, the pack goes from two legs to four, but feast upon flesh of your own and you will change no more.* 'He wants to coax Madeleine, then eat her, doesn't he?' I say. 'He wants to take the pack full wolf? He's going to kill her.'

Gerald looks away. Terror and anger rip through my body and come out as a scream in a voice I don't even recognise. 'She's a baby. A baby,' I sob. 'We have to stop him.'

I glance back and notice something at the window.

The creature's long nose, white teeth and red eyes don't disguise who it is.

'Lily,' I say.

'Why is *she* here?' she asks Gerald, climbing down into the room.

Last time I saw Lily in wolf form I didn't have time to take in what she looked like. Her hair is a beautiful brown. She looks amazing, a million miles from the shy girl who hides behind her own hair. She swishes her tail confidently and steps forward.

'Oberon is serious about taking the pack full wolf,' Gerald says. 'He's taken Madeleine with him to use as the sacrifice.'

'But she isn't related to you. Will isn't her father,' I say. 'He'll just kill her for no good reason.'

Gerald nods to indicate that I'm telling the truth.

'We have to stop him,' I say again.

Lily turns to me. 'This is wolf business,' she says. '*You're* not going to do anything.'

'How come you're here anyway?' I say. 'I thought Father Gowlett was babysitting for you?'

'He left,' Lily says impatiently.

'He left you when he was supposed to be baby-sitting?'

Lily looks at me. 'Do I look like a baby that needs sitting?'

'What happened?' asks Gerald.

'He told us that he knows about us. He was really

creepy, saying stuff like we could open up to him about our secrets. He said whatever we said he would understand and he'd help us. It was pretty obvious what he was doing. He wants to show us off like animals he has discovered.'

'But you won't let him, will you?'

'Elspeth told him she would. She told him to meet her in the woods where she would let him take her picture. We have to find her before she does something stupid.'

'You mean she's going to kill him,' I say.

Lily's eyes answer the question. 'Tonight is full moon when the wolf's voice is loudest.'

'You'll have to get Freddie's help,' Gerald says to Lily. 'I've got to bring Madeleine back.'

'I'll help,' I say.

Lily raises her nose close to my face, pushing me backwards out of the room. 'You stay here,' she says. 'This is nothing to do with you.' I haven't heard her speak like this. She sounds angry, dangerous. She slams the bedroom door in my face. I try the handle but the door won't open. I bang on it.

'Let me in. I can help,' I yell. I try the handle again and the door flies open; they have both gone.

Overhead, a cloud drifts past the moon. The hill with Percy's Ruin is visible from where I am standing. There is a flickering flame at the top. I think of little Madeleine somewhere up there in the woods with Oberon.

There's a phone in the hallway but I can't call for help as I don't have anyone's number. Next to it is Uncle Will's bicycle. I grab it and head downstairs. The bike is awkward on the stairs and the pedals keep bashing my shins, but I get it out and the front door slams shut behind me. Madeleine is all that matters now. All these cousins and uncles related by blood and it turns out that the one I care about most isn't actually a relative at all.

21
THE SILVER BULLET TECHNIQUE

The well-lit streets give way to dark windy uphill lanes. Even in the lowest gear the climb towards Percy's Ruin is hard on my legs. Each time a car passes me, the headlights throw shadows into the surrounding woods. I have never felt such fear. My hands are like ice. My body is numbed by the cold. The only thing that stops me from turning the bike around and freewheeling back into town is the thought of Madeleine.

A car passes, then suddenly stops and reverses along the road. It stops on the verge and the door opens. A figure steps out. It's too dark to see who it is but I know the moment he speaks.

'Mariel? What brings you out tonight? It's not safe for you,' says Father Gowlett.

'Nor you,' I reply.

'I've arranged to meet with Elspeth in the woods so I can get my evidence.'

'She'll kill you. They've always known about you. It was Flora that kept you safe,' I reply.

The red glow from the car's backlights gives his face a demonic look. There is a strange look in his eyes, a mixture of fear and excitement. 'I think I have a fair chance of survival.' He opens the boot of his car and takes out a leather travel bag. He unzips it. It is full of silver jewellery. He reaches into the boot again and pulls out a camera and then his rifle.

'You're planning to shoot her?'

'Of course I would much rather your cousins willingly gave themselves up. But if they refuse to let the world in on their secret then this is the only way. A wounded wolf is a dangerous creature. A dead werewolf, on the other hand, is a brilliant prize.'

'She's a little girl.'

'Elspeth is no little girl tonight. She's an animal. Some of us are made in God's image, but your cousins are not. They are something very different. No one will judge me for sacrificing her life in order to show the world of the existence of these creatures and for revealing the true beasts of Wilderdale.'

'You must go back. She will kill you.'

'An eight-year-old wolfling against me with a bag of silver and a shotgun. We'll see who gets hurt.' He flips the barrel and loads the gun. 'Ever heard of silver bullets killing werewolves?'

'Is it true?'

'No. Any old bullet shot through the heart will kill a werewolf. The silver bullet is a technique. It's a method passed down through generations of wolf hunters. To kill a wolf stay hidden, stay still and silently wait, then set your sights at the heart and aim straight. To make a mistake, will seal your fate. Any metal will do for the bullet, the silver is used for the bait.'

'You lure them with silver,' I say.

He holds the barrel of his gun up and looks through the sight. 'They can't resist it. And tonight, with the moon full they are at their most careless.'

'Where are you meeting her?'

'At the same spot I saw Flora all those years ago.'

'How can you think of killing one of them? How can you? You preach about believing in God and being nice to everyone. How can you do something like this?'

Father Gowlett touches his dog collar. 'This is God's most important work. I am ridding the earth of the devil's creation.'

'But it's a gene. You said so yourself.'

'It's a genetic defect and one which I believe can be traced back to the father of evil himself. But you haven't answered my question. What brings you out tonight, Mariel?'

I tell him about Oberon taking Madeleine. He doesn't say anything in response but reaches into the bag of jewellery and takes out a silver cross just like the one I found by Percy's Ruin. He hands it to me. It glints in the moonlight.

'I swore to your grandfather I would protect you but perhaps both of our fates await us in the woods tonight,' he says.

'Why did you say you'd protect me?'

'That's how Frank died, protecting you. Flora was going to kill you.'

'Why would she have killed me?'

'It's what they do. They're killers. You can have no sympathy for any of them.'

He pulls out his keys and locks the car. It beeps twice and the lights go off, leaving us with the milky white light of the full moon. I have one more question before he leaves.

'Is there any chance . . . I mean, is there any danger I'm one of them?'

'Thankfully no. The gene is very specific. It can only be passed down through carriers of the opposite sex from the parent wolf. There is no way you could be infected any more than I could.'

'Last night I dreamed I was one of them.'

'Dreams have no meaning, Mariel. Good luck.'

I watch him disappear into the woods, then I get back on the bike and cycle further up the road. I get as near to Percy's Ruin as I can, then lean the bike against a tree and continue on foot up through the forest. The ground is soft and damp. The cold wind whistles through the trees. Every branch sways. Every twig shakes. Everything moves. My imagination conjures up things from the shadows but what could be scarier than the truth that awaits me?

On top of the hill, Percy's Ruin is partly illuminated by the moonlight. A fire burns at the top. Halfway up, where the wall has crumbled and fallen away, there is a bundle of blankets. From the piercing screams that fill the air I can tell this is Madeleine.

Below are three wolves. I approach behind a fallen tree trunk. Oberon and Freddie are facing each other menacingly. They have been fighting. Freddie is walking with a limp and Oberon has a gash on his back. I head around the hill towards the tower and spot Amelia standing by its entrance. It's the first time I have seen her in wolf form. Her model's cheekbones are now stretched and lined with soft brown hair. Somehow she's still beautiful.

I hear Oberon say, 'You can't defeat me. You must accept me as pack leader.'

'I can't accept going full wolf,' replies Freddie. 'Amelia, you don't want this, do you?'

'We have to follow the pack leader. It's what Ma'wolf taught us,' she replies.

'You can't make us do it just because your life as a human sucks,' says Freddie angrily. 'Madeleine's our cousin too. It's not just up to you what happens to her.'

'Then perhaps I'll pick you as our sacrifice,' replies Oberon. He jumps forward, snapping his jaws at Freddie. Freddie ducks but not fast enough. Oberon nips his shoulder, then licks the blood from his teeth.

'Accept it, Freddie, I'm stronger, I'm quicker, I'm better.'

I need to get Amelia away from the entrance to the tower. I reach into my pocket and feel the cold metal of the silver cross. I have one chance to make this work. I position myself behind a tree, then throw the cross into some bushes away from the tower. I look around the tree and see that she has taken the bait. She gets up and walks away from the tower, sniffing out the silver cross.

Quickly, I climb over the fence and run to the tower, through the doorway, up the stairs. Madeleine's cries sound desperate and scared. Her voice echoes off the tower walls. She is thrashing her arms and legs around hysterically and has managed to kick off the blankets. Her pink sleepsuit is grubby and she's shivering. I pick her up. Her skin feels like ice. I hold her tightly to warm her up. She stops crying. I run back downstairs but before I reach the doorway I hear a voice at the bottom.

'Hello, cuz,' says Oberon.

I step out of the tower to find Amelia, Oberon and Freddie staring at me. I cling tightly to Madeleine.

'Mariel, you shouldn't be out tonight,' says Amelia.

'That's right,' snarls Oberon. 'I warned you what would happen to you if you came out.'

Freddie steps in his way. 'Leave her alone,' he growls.

'Why? Because you want to protect her or are you too scared to act like a real wolf and kill her?' replies Oberon.

Freddie lunges at Oberon but is knocked sideways and lets out a howl of pain.

'I will not let you lead us down a path that takes us full wolf,' says Freddie.

'No one is going full wolf tonight,' says a voice.

It's Gerald. He steps out into the clearing. As a wolf he has a powerful stride, and like Lily he is much more confident than he is as a human.

'Ah, decided to join us at last, have you, bro?' says Oberon.

'Gowlett is in the woods. Elspeth plans to kill him,' he replies.

'Let her,' says Oberon.

'If she kills a human, she'll be a challenger for the leadership,' says Gerald.

'That's true,' says Amelia.

Oberon pauses. 'OK, we'll stop her but what about those two?' Oberon nods his head in my direction.

'I'll watch them until you return,' says Gerald. 'The rest of you can go and find Elspeth.'

Oberon's eyes narrow. 'You sure you're not going to wimp out on me and let them go?' he says.

'No, she's seen too much. She can't live to see daylight,' replies Gerald.

'Now you're talking my language,' says Oberon with a triumphant laugh. 'But just in case you have a change of heart . . .' He swings around suddenly and lunges towards me. Pain shoots through my leg. I scream and fall to my knees, still desperately clutching Madeleine. I look up to see blood dripping from Oberon's mouth. He has taken a bite out of my leg. The pain is unbelievable.

'You idiot,' snarls Gerald. 'She needs to die without it looking suspicious.'

'Watch who you're calling an idiot, bro. I may be younger but I'm the leader of this pack now. Come on, let's stop Elspeth doing anything silly. Keep an eye on them,' says Oberon, leading the others down into the woods.

22

FIVE BITES

Gerald approaches. 'You shouldn't have come.'

He moves forward and takes Madeleine's blankets between his teeth. Carefully he picks her up. She starts to cry again.

I try to stand but the leg Oberon wounded gives way. 'Take me too,' I beg.

'I can only take one of you,' he replies.

I want desperately to be saved but, looking at Madeleine's face, so young and untouched by life, I know there is no choice.

He places her gently in front of me.

'Say goodbye,' he says. 'I'm sorry, Mariel. I hope your death is as painless as possible.'

Gerald picks her up and walks away.

I am alone. Tears blur my vision. I look up at the moon. A halo of light surrounds it. It pulsates with energy. It is so beautiful it makes me smile. I think I understand how it can wield so much power over my cousins. The intensity of it burns my eyes. It calls me.

A ripping pain brings me out of my trance. Blood oozes from a fresh wound on my other leg. Lily is standing in front of me, her intense brown eyes lowering to my level. There is blood on her teeth from the bite.

'Why?' I ask.

'I need your help,' she replies.

'I'm not sure . . . you're going the right . . . way about getting it.' The joke sounds weak, the emphasis on the words is all wrong.

She lurches forwards and bites my arm.

'Why are you doing this? I thought you wanted my help.'

'The first bite for the blood to appear, the second for the pain and for the tears, the third and fourth cause anger and fear.'

'But I'm not a Considine. The gene only passes through male parents.'

'Look at your hand. A few days ago Elspeth scratched you but there's no trace of it now. You have healing skin like us.'

I look at my hand. She's right. It has healed. It never seemed strange because scratches and cuts have always healed fast. I've never known any different and Mum has never paid enough attention to notice.

'The diary you found wasn't Grandma's,' says Lily.

'She knew it was in the house but she didn't know where he hid it.'

'Who?'

'Our grandad.'

'I don't understand.'

'Grandad was a wolf too. The diary explains it all. His family had run here for generations until Ma'wolf came to Wilderdale. She married him and joined his pack. She killed the pack leader, Grandad's grandad. That was Percy, who built this tower. She made it look as though he jumped from the top but she killed him.'

Lily lunges and bites my other leg. I scream. I try to take in what she is saying but the pain is confusing me. 'You mean I'm like you?'

She nods. 'Grandad wanted to save you from this life so he sent you away, but Ma'wolf wanted her pack. She would have coaxed you when you were old enough. That's why she killed him.'

Blood gushes out. It reddens my clothes. 'I don't want this,' I say.

'You don't have a choice. You're bleeding to death. Our skin is self-healing. This is the only way to save you.' She bites into my side. 'The fifth must be felt for the wolf to be here.'

My head feels heavy. The sound of the trees in the wind grows louder. It's like the whistling wind is whispering to me, whistling one word over and over again. Wolf . . . wolf . . . wolf. My pain turns to agony.

Something is growing inside me. My bones are altering, changing, taking on a new form.

'What's happening to me?'

It is my voice that asks the question but I know the answer. I am standing on all fours. I look down at a muddy puddle and see the reflection of my changed face. My chin is longer, my nose is black. Hair has sprouted at the edges. My ears have become elongated. And yet it does not feel like I am staring at a stranger's face. There is a part of me that has always known about this. The part I left each night in the dreams I didn't remember. The part that led me out of bed at night. It's the part of me that wanted this to happen, the part that was waiting impatiently for this to happen.

I look up at the moon. It is full and beautiful, like music is radiating from it. And inside my head I hear the voice, loud and clear. *Kill kill kill,* it says.

I shake off the remains of my clothes, desperate to be free of them. Something stirs within. Hunger like I have never felt before: hunger for life, hunger for the living, hunger for death. I desire flesh between my teeth, blood on my tongue, meat in my throat. I want bone and gristle to fill my empty stomach.

I can smell potential food everywhere. Something moves nearby. I dive into the bush and grab it in my jaws. In the moonlight I see it is a rabbit. I rip into it instinctively, tearing off its fur. It is as though I have spent my life in starvation until this point.

When I have stripped every scrap of meat from the bones, Lily says, 'It's time to go. We can still save Gowlett.'

'They're meeting where he saw Ma'wolf change,' I say.

'Follow me,' she replies. 'And be careful. This is your first change and the moon is full. You need to remember yourself.'

As I follow her through the woods, I find it easy to keep up. My limbs feel full of energy. All pain has gone. My wounds have healed. My mind has altered too. Everything is instinct. Emotions have receded. Smells and sounds have changed. My nose can detect the living creatures of the forest, scurrying around me, burrowing beneath me, but I cannot tell what they are. All flesh smells the same. All flesh smells sweet. *Kill kill kill*, says the voice.

We reach a clearing with a hollowed-out tree trunk at its centre. Something on the grass catches my eye. It glints in the moonlight. It's something I want. It's there just for me. It's mine. I run to it, keen to claim my prize before Lily sees it.

'Mariel, come back.'

Lily's voice is distant. I am focused on the object. It is a silver bangle. It is the most beautiful thing I have ever seen. I bend down to pick it up in my mouth. I hear a click. I look up and there is a *bang* and a flash of light, followed by a deep burning pain in my knee. I look down at the wound. I've been shot. The force of the bullet knocks me over. My scream comes out as a howl.

I can feel the bullet pressed up against the mangled inside of my knee. The bone has been shattered. I tense the muscles around it, trying to squeeze it out.

Lying with my head on the ground I see Father Gowlett step out of the hollow tree. His shotgun is still smoking. He hurries towards me and takes aim again, but he stops and lowers his gun.

'Mariel?'

'The silver bullet technique,' I reply with a smile.

Father Gowlett looks at me with an expression on his face I don't fully understand, then he cries out and falls. I raise my head to see Lily. She has jumped on him and kicked his gun away. She grabs the camera strap from his other shoulder, tears it off him and bites through the camera, spitting bits of it out.

'We came to rescue you, you stupid man,' she says.

'I just wanted evidence. I meant you no harm.'

'That's why you came out here with a gun?' She is the angriest I have seen her.

'I just wanted people to believe me.'

Lily growls at him.

I try to understand what they are saying but it seems far away, unreal, like it doesn't concern me, like the volume is too low. All my energy is focused on the bullet I am forcing out of my body.

I hear Elspeth's voice. 'Some men will come to seek us, all they want is proof, but if they succeed and see us, the last thing they'll see is wolf.'

'No, Elspeth. This has gone far enough,' says Lily.

'I'm your pack leader,' says Oberon. 'I'll decide.'

I look up and see that Elspeth, Freddie and Amelia are there too, everyone except Gerald.

'It's not in our interests to kill the priest,' says Lily.

'I'm interested in it,' replies Oberon. 'But first let's have a look at this beautiful creature.'

He is talking about me. My cousins approach.

Freddie smiles. 'How is this possible?'

'Grandad had the gene,' says Lily.

'Another member for our pack,' says Freddie.

'Mariel, we can have so much fun,' says Amelia.

'She's from a different line. She should run alone,' says Elspeth.

'No. She is wounded. This is the sacrifice that will enable us to go full wolf,' Oberon says.

I feel my tissue and bone healing fast but it hurts and I can't defend myself.

'I think we can find someone better to feast on than her,' says Freddie.

Oberon swings round to face him. Freddie is crouching down. He has Father's Gowlett's gun. It looks awkward to hold but he is managing to point it at Oberon's chest, his claw on the trigger.

'Don't be stupid, Freddie,' says Oberon.

'Don't call me stupid,' says Freddie.

'Or what? You'll shoot me?'

'If I have to.'

Oberon moves towards him threateningly. 'Go on then,' he says. 'I dare you.'

There is a loud *bang* and something hits my eye. I wipe it away and look at my paw. There is blood on it. Oberon is lying utterly still on his back. He's dead. The hair that covers his body begins to vanish, sinking back into the pores of his skin quickly until he is a naked boy with a bloody hole in his chest.

'What have you done?' utters Father Gowlett.

'You've killed him,' Elspeth says. There is no emotion in her voice.

I feel no pity either. I understand what has happened but I don't feel angry or upset. Finally the bullet drops out of my knee and my wound is able to heal over. I lick the blood off the bullet until it shines pleasingly in the moonlight. I stand on all fours. It feels like it's the only way to stand. I look at Oberon's dead body. Once I would have cared. Not now. Now, it is just another kill.

'Don't you understand what you've done? You've killed your own cousin,' says Father Gowlett.

I feel like laughing at the horror in his voice.

'There's no such thing as a bad kill,' replies Freddie triumphantly.

'It was you,' says Father Gowlett, pointing at Freddie,

his voice trembling with fear. 'You killed Flora, didn't you?'

Freddie laughs. 'I killed Ma'wolf and I killed Oberon.' He turns to us. 'Anyone else want to stand in my way of being the leader?'

Elspeth sniggers. 'The killer kills, because death must be fed, the killer kills till all are dead, the killer kills and so it's said, that by the killer we all are led.'

'But why?' asks Father Gowlett.

'Ambition to lead,' replies Freddie. 'That's how it is with the wolf. Power is everything.'

'And how are you going to explain this? Have you thought about that?' demands Lily. She snarls at Freddie. I struggle to understand her anger.

Freddie looks down at the gun, then up at Father Gowlett. 'We'll let the vicar go,' he says.

'How will that help?' asks Amelia.

'Oberon was shot by a bullet from Gowlett's gun with his fingerprints on it.'

'They can tell who has shot the gun?' says Lily.

'He did shoot the gun. He shot me,' I say.

'Exactly. And claws don't leave prints,' says Freddie.

'You killed him. Not me,' protests Father Gowlett.

'Try explaining that to the police. Excuse me, officer, a werewolf did it.' Freddie laughs.

'I will tell the truth.'

'So they'll lock you up in a lunatic asylum rather

than a prison. Now, I'm offering you your life. It's the best offer you'll get. I suggest you take it.'

'Run or be killed,' whispers Elspeth.

Father Gowlett turns and runs full pelt down the hill.

Freddie throws his head back and lets out a howl from the back of his throat that speaks to me in a wordless language that travels straight to my soul. It is like he's calling me. He is channelling me. The others join in. The noise overwhelms me. It inspires me. It consumes me. It is beautiful and strong. I want to be a part of it. I want to be a part of them. I throw my head back and howl too. I feel at peace. Our howls harmonise with nature. I stare at the moon and feel its power. It's as though it is pouring into me, filling me up with its goodness and strength.

I don't know how long we howl for but we stop when Gerald arrives. He nudges Oberon's lifeless body with his nose, confirming he is dead.

'I killed him,' says Freddie.

Gerald looks at me, eyeing my wolf's body.

'How did this happen?'

'Save your explanations,' says Freddie. 'We need to move quickly now. Where's Madeleine?'

'I took her home,' replies Gerald. 'The police were there. They must have come back and found us missing. I left her in one of the police cars. No one saw me.'

'We need to return to our houses,' says Amelia.

'It's too late for that,' says Elspeth. 'Soon they'll come looking for us.'

'They'll have called the others,' says Lily. 'Even if we blame Father Gowlett for Oberon's death, what would we give as our reason for coming out at night? They'll separate us.'

'It's time,' whispers Elspeth excitedly.

'What does our new leader say?' asks Lily.

Freddie looks at each one of us in turn. He paces, deep in thought. I know what he is thinking and I know what I want him to say. Finally he speaks. 'I am your leader and tonight I will lead you to completion, then we will find new places to run where we will be safe and free and wild.'

'It's time,' says Elspeth again.

'We have no choice,' says Freddie. 'Tonight we go full wolf.'

'I agree. It's the only option,' says Gerald.

'Me too,' says Amelia.

Lily takes the longest to answer but eventually she nods and says, 'Full wolf.'

'We change no more, no more life's lie, no weak human hearts, we're wolves till we die,' says Elspeth.

'What about you, Mariel?' says Freddie.

My leg is totally healed now. I feel strong and power-ful. *Kill kill kill*, says the voice. I try to remember my life before the change. I try to remember when life was just Mum and me living in Australia. It doesn't seem real to me any more. *Kill kill kill,* says the voice. I understand that if I choose this life, my mother will spend the rest of hers wondering what happened to me. I will never kiss a boy or go to university or get a job or get married. But the life before me, in the light of the full moon, seems richer and more exciting than anything else I could choose.

If I go back, I will live each day as a lie. A vegetarian by day, a carnivore by night. I would be torn apart by the two voices. My human self would fear my wolf side. The wolf would despise the human.

'Choose,' urges Elspeth.

There are two paths before me. One is full of lies and self-loathing. The other is pure, honest and instinctive. My life has always been lies. I breathe the cold winter air into my lungs and feel the reality of what is about to happen. To live life pretending these feelings don't exist is unbearable. There really is only one answer.

'Full wolf,' I say.

We all stand over Oberon's dead body. The ground around him has reddened from his blood.

We all know what we must do. My mouth waters in anticipation of the flesh. I look from cousin to cousin, from wolf to wolf. There is no doubt left. We lower our heads and open our jaws to sink our teeth into Oberon's flesh.

When we are finished, Freddie howls and runs into

the woods. We follow. He knows where to take us. He will keep us safe.

Finally I am somewhere I belong.

Happily I run with the pack.

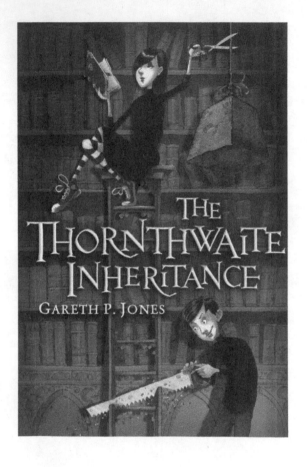